MORRIS GLEITZMAN

ARISTOTLE'S NOSTRIL

Puffin Books

PUFFIN BOOKS

UK | USA | Canada | Ireland | Australia
India | New Zealand | South Africa | China

Penguin Books is part of the Penguin Random House group of companies
whose addresses can be found at global.penguinrandomhouse.com.

First published by Penguin Australia Pty Ltd, 2005
This edition published by Penguin Australia Pty Ltd, 2016

1 3 5 7 9 10 8 6 4 2

Cover design by Tony Palmer © Penguin Australia Pty Ltd, 2016
Cover illustration copyright Jeremy Ley, 2016
Typeset in Minion by Post Pre-press Group, Brisbane, Queensland
Colour separation by Splitting Image Colour Studio, Clayton, Victoria
Printed and bound in Australia by Griffin Press, an accredited ISO AS/NZS 14001
Environmental Management Systems printer.

National Library of Australia Cataloguing-in-Publication data:
Gleitzman, Morris, 1953- author.
Aristotle's Nostril / Morris Gleitzman.
ISBN: 978 0 14 330894 2 (paperback)
For children.
Subjects: Happiness – Juvenile fiction.
Children's stories.
A823.3

puffin.com.au

ARISTOTLE'S NOSTRIL

Also by Morris Gleitzman

*For Sarah, Trudi, Katie, Emily, Jessica, Kellie,
Daniel, Laura, Maddie and Grace*

1

Aristotle's whole body went grin-shaped as he thought about the good thing he was going to do.

He knew if the other nose germs found out, they'd think it was a naughty thing.

Very naughty.

They might even punish him.

Aristotle didn't care.

I'll just have to make sure they don't catch me, he thought.

He peered around the crowded floor of the nostril and up the vast teeming nostril walls to the heavily-populated nostril ceiling high above. Nobody was watching. The other germs were all having a meeting. Something about a new law to ban germs giving other germs piggybacks.

This was the perfect moment.

Aristotle crept over to Blob, grabbed him and dragged him behind a chunk of broken-off nose hair.

'Hey,' complained Blob. 'Don't. I'm trying to count how many germs are at the meeting. Now I can't remember if I was up to six million and thirty-seven or six million and thirty-eight.'

'Surprise,' said Aristotle happily.

He pointed to the cake sitting on a pimple.

Blob stopped struggling.

Aristotle felt himself go grin-shaped again.

I'm a very lucky germ, he thought. I've got a brother who likes having fun as much as I do. Well, almost as much. Well, a bit. Well, he will when he tastes the cake.

Blob was staring at the white fluffy icing and the ten flickering candles.

'What is it?' he said, puzzled.

For a moment Aristotle thought Blob was joking. Then he remembered his brother never joked. Plus Blob's normally round body was scrunched flat with disapproval. He looked more like a skin flake than a germ.

'It's a birthday cake,' said Aristotle. 'It's what germs in exotic foreign places give each other on their birthdays.'

Blob looked long-sufferingly at Aristotle.

'By exotic foreign places,' said Blob, 'I assume you mean places outside the nostril?'

'Yes,' said Aristotle.

He knew why Blob was looking disapproving. Blob didn't like anything from outside the nostril. Aristotle couldn't understand why. Blob had never

2

been outside the nostril, none of them had, so why was he so picky?

Aristotle didn't let it spoil his birthday mood.

'The cake's not from outside the nostril,' he said. 'Just the recipe. I got it from a visitor. Happy birthday, Blob.'

Aristotle waited hopefully for Blob to relax and grin back and give him a hug. He'd often wondered what it would be like to be hugged, to be wrapped up in all of Blob's arms and several of his legs.

But Blob wasn't relaxing.

Or grinning.

Or hugging.

Blob was folding most of his arms, which made him look like an angry adult. Aristotle always felt sad to see kids carrying on like adults. Around here young germs did that a lot.

'We germs don't have birthdays,' said Blob sternly. 'You know that. We don't live long enough. You've got to live at least a year to have a birthday.'

Aristotle sighed.

'Blob,' he pleaded. 'This is our anniversary. We're ten. We were born ten hours ago. We should be celebrating.'

'Are you crazy?' said Blob. He glanced anxiously up at the nose-hair highway overhead to see if anyone was watching. 'Do you know how many laws we'd be breaking? The No Parties part of the Nostril Protection Act for a start.'

Aristotle felt his excitement and pleasure draining away.

'You're already violating the Fluffy Icing Prohibition Bill,' continued Blob. 'Which is a law, as you know very well, that specifically forbids, anywhere in this nostril, the making of fluffy icing.'

'It's just mashed skin flakes,' said Aristotle. 'Please, Blob, blow out the candles. Have some fun, just for once.'

'I will do no such thing,' said Blob. 'These candles are in direct contravention of the Nasal Passage Fire Control Act.'

'They're not real candles,' sighed Aristotle. 'They're just some carbon molecules that I know burning off a bit of energy as a favour.'

Blob peered at the carbon molecules more closely. The carbon molecules gave him a cheery wave. Blob jumped back, alarmed.

'Get rid of them now,' he said. 'And the icing, and the cake. Do you have any idea what will happen if the authorities see this cake?'

'They'll want a piece?' said Aristotle hopefully.

'A piece of you is what they'll want,' snapped Blob.

Aristotle looked sadly at his brother. How could his very own identical twin be so different to him?

We both look the same, he thought. We both have exactly the same round bodies. We both have exactly the same number of arms and legs, with all the arms at the top and all the legs at the bottom.

4

But we aren't the same.

'Blob,' said Aristotle quietly. 'Why don't you want to be happy?'

Blob's whole body went grim-shaped.

'We're not here to be happy,' he said. 'We're here to make sure the nostril operates in an orderly and efficient manner.'

Aristotle wanted to grab Blob and shake him till his insides wobbled. He wanted to ask him what made a kid of ten talk like some ancient ninety-six-hour-old.

He didn't.

A loud voice was suddenly echoing across the nostril.

'What's going on over there?' it boomed.

Aristotle and Blob shrank down behind the chunk of nose hair.

'We've had it now,' moaned Blob. 'We'll be up for disciplinary action and smacked bottoms.'

'Come out immediately,' boomed the voice. 'And bring that illegal cake with you.'

Blob went sag-shaped. He put all his hands up and stepped miserably out from the hiding place.

Aristotle picked up the cake and followed.

He tried not to think about what would happen now. The anger. The punishment. The blowing up of the cake by the cake-disposal squad.

At least Blob wouldn't be blamed. The authorities would say it was all Aristotle's fault, and they'd be right.

He was the odd germ out.

He was the one who'd been born with the tragic and mysterious problem.

Why am I so different, thought Aristotle sadly. Why am I, out of all the millions and millions of germs in the nostril, the only one who wants to be happy?

2

Court was in session.

'The defendant is charged,' said the clerk of the court, 'with being in possession of an illegal item, namely a birthday cake, and attempting to have fun with it.'

Aristotle didn't like being in court.

He was used to it. He'd been in front of the court more times than he could remember. The judges' seats, ornate and high-backed and carved out of priceless ancient dried phlegm, were quite familiar. So were the judges' wigs, woven from real dust-mite armpit hair. But Aristotle still found the whole experience scary.

The judges were so strict.

And the jury was so big.

Aristotle gazed up at the towering sides of the nostril, at the huge nose-hair highways criss-crossing the nostril airspace, at the vast military camps high up under the nostril roof. From every

7

part of the nostril millions of germs were glaring down at him. Most of them seemed to be angrily waving their arms and legs.

I could be wrong about that, thought Aristotle hopefully. It could just be the wind. It's pretty strong up there and it could just be making their limbs flap.

'Defendant,' boomed the chief judge. 'How do you plead?'

Aristotle turned back to the judges. At least there were only a few hundred of them. Unfortunately they looked even angrier than the jury.

The warm outgoing wind died away and the nostril was suddenly filled with the cold rush of incoming wind.

Aristotle shivered.

'Guilty or not guilty?' boomed the chief judge.

This was always the tricky part. There wasn't much point pleading not guilty when the court had three million witnesses. But Aristotle hated pleading guilty. He didn't feel guilty. Scared, yes, but not guilty.

'It was only a birthday cake,' he said.

Millions of voices murmured disapprovingly from above.

The judges and the jury all went grim-shaped. The whole nostril was silent for a moment except for the faint sound of incoming dust chunks bouncing off nose-hair highways and jury members.

Aristotle, looking up again, saw that hurtling

in with the dust chunks was a new visitor. An exotic spiral-shaped microbe with multi-coloured tentacles, which were flapping helplessly as the wind carried the microbe towards the back of the nostril.

Aristotle knew it wouldn't get there.

It didn't.

Members of the nostril defence force, airborne division, swung down from the roof on ropes, snatched the exotic microbe out of the airstream and dragged it away.

Poor thing, thought Aristotle. Now it'll end up in court too.

Aristotle realised that Blob, who was standing next to him in the dock, had shuffled closer.

'Plead guilty,' muttered Blob. 'Don't make it worse by lying. I'll give you the usual character reference. The one where I explain to them that you're basically a decent germ but also a bit of an idiot.'

Aristotle gave Blob a grateful look.

Honest and generous. What more could a germ ask for in a brother? Apart from happy.

But before Aristotle could enter a plea, the chief judge did it for him.

'You've already admitted you had a birthday cake on or about your person,' said the chief judge. 'That sounds guilty to me.'

'Fair enough,' said Aristotle quietly.

The germ multitudes muttered disapprovingly again.

'Before I pass sentence,' said the chief judge, 'I wish to make a few remarks.'

Aristotle wasn't surprised. The chief judge always made a few remarks at this point in Aristotle's trials.

'We live in the most important part of the human body,' said the chief judge. 'Not in an arm or a leg or a . . . or a . . .'

The chief judge looked around at the other judges for help.

Aristotle sighed. The chief judge always did this, ran out of names for the parts of the human body. Why couldn't he just admit that he didn't know? And that none of the other germs in the nostril did either?

'Beak,' said one of the judges.

'Fin,' said another.

'Brightly-coloured external bottom flap,' said a third.

'Exactly,' said the chief judge. 'We don't live in any of those bits. We live in the nostril. The human body only has one nostril, and we have a sacred duty to make sure it operates in an orderly and efficient manner. If we lived in a leg, things would be different. Everyone knows a human has more than one leg.'

'Seven,' said one of the judges.

'Thirty-two,' said another.

'Exactly,' said the chief judge. 'And four big toes and two tummies and quite a few wings.'

'And,' chimed in another judge, 'several brightly-coloured external bottom flaps.'

Aristotle sighed again. If the chief judge and the other authorities bothered talking to the airborne visiting microbes instead of just locking them up, the chief judge would know that humans had ten big toes, three tummies and very rarely a beak.

'But this isn't any of those other body parts.' The chief judge was still on his favourite topic. 'This is the nostril. The sacred, precious, one-of-a-kind nostril. And the nostril of a human is not the place for fun, games, silliness or birthday cakes.'

Pity, thought Aristotle. I reckon this place would run much more efficiently if everyone relaxed a bit.

He realised the chief judge was looking at him.

So was everybody else.

'Sorry,' said Aristotle. 'I'll try not to be silly in future.'

He meant it, he really did. Right now he'd give anything to be a normal law-abiding germ. One who wasn't about to be sentenced to an unpleasant few minutes of snot sweeping.

'I wish I could believe you,' said the chief judge, suddenly going even grimmer-shaped than before. 'But how many times has this court heard you say that in the past?'

Aristotle didn't know.

'Clerk, if you please,' said the chief judge.

The clerk of the court stepped forward, fluttering all his arms importantly.

'The defendant,' he said, 'was first found guilty of

being silly when he used a snot dollop as a bouncy castle.'

'Not a bouncy castle, your honour,' said Aristotle quietly. 'A trampoline.'

The chief judge glared at Aristotle.

'The defendant was next found guilty of being silly,' said the clerk, 'when he smeared Highway 42 with nostril grease and slid down it on his bottom.'

'I explained about that in court at the time,' said Aristotle. 'I didn't do any smearing, it was already greasy.'

'Then,' said the clerk, 'the defendant . . .'

'Just the total,' said the chief judge.

'Yes, your honour,' said the clerk, giving the chief judge a hurt look. 'The defendant has been convicted of sixty-three other silliness offences, and two hundred and fourteen counts of spending time with other silly individuals.'

'Thank you,' said the chief judge.

Aristotle protested.

'The microbes from outside aren't silly,' he said. 'They're just a bit dazed from being blown in here by the wind. But they know heaps of interesting stuff. How to play chess and do bungy-jumping. How to make sports equipment out of skin flakes. I met one who can play music on hollow lumps of dust-mite poo.'

'Enough,' boomed the chief judge. He glowered down at Aristotle. 'Young germ, I think you can see why the birthday cake is the last straw and why we have to make an example of you.'

Aristotle suddenly felt a chill, even though the wind had just changed again and warm air was gusting out through the nostril.

What did the judge mean?

'Before you pass sentence, your honour,' said Aristotle, 'can I have a witness in my defence?'

The chief judge nodded wearily.

Aristotle looked at Blob.

Blob was gazing up at the jury members, counting them.

'One million and one...one million and two...'

Aristotle gave him a nudge.

Blob jumped, looked around and saw the judges staring at him.

'Sorry,' he said. 'Um...character reference... right. Well, I've known my brother Aristotle for a long time, ten hours in fact, and um...well... there's obviously something very wrong with him, but...er...I don't know what it is and I don't think he can help it.'

Aristotle felt very moved.

Poor Blob hated public speaking and here he was, twisting himself into knots with stress, the only germ in the whole place prepared to offer Aristotle support.

Suddenly Aristotle didn't feel so tragic after all.

I've got a brother who loves me, he thought, and

a nostril to call home. Nothing's more important than that.

The judges all stood up.

'Taking into account,' said the chief judge to Aristotle, 'that you clearly do have something wrong with you, and that nobody seems to know how to cure your silliness, including your brother and partner in crime, the sentence of the court is as follows.'

Aristotle gave Blob a grateful look.

Thanks to him, the sentence looked like it was going to be a light one.

'You and your brother will both leave the nostril right now,' said the chief judge, 'and never come back.'

3

Banished.

Aristotle didn't even want to think about the word.

But he couldn't help it because as he and Blob trudged slowly and miserably towards the nostril exit, millions of nose germs kept yelling it at them.

'Banished.'

'Banished.'

'You are so banished.'

Aristotle trudged on, trying to ignore the voices.

It wasn't easy. Even the platoon of nostril defence force soldiers escorting them were muttering it.

It got a bit easier after a while when all the civilian germs stopped yelling and went back to their meeting. They were passing a new law banning tickling and handstands.

The platoon commander ordered the soldiers to be quiet, and then all Aristotle could hear was Blob.

'Why me?' wailed Blob, waving all his arms and several of his legs. 'I'm innocent. Why send me away?'

Aristotle felt awful.

Poor Blob.

Aristotle had tried to explain to the judges that Blob was completely innocent, that he hadn't asked for any of the things Aristotle had given him – not the birthday cake, the trampoline or the bungy-jumping rope made out of the stretchy bit from under a flea's tongue.

But the judges hadn't listened.

'It's not fair,' wailed Blob.

I've got to do something, thought Aristotle miserably. Find some way of keeping us here so Blob doesn't have to leave all the other nose germs he loves to count so much.

Aristotle thought about grabbing Blob and them both running for it and hiding out in an abandoned mucus mine.

Silly idea.

Aristotle knew from painful experience that nose germs had too many legs to run fast. If they tried, they got all tangled up and fell in a heap. The best they could do was trot. And right now he and Blob were being marched away by troops who could almost certainly trot faster than them.

'I'm a tragic victim of injustice,' moaned Blob.

Suddenly Aristotle saw something that gave him a glimmer of hope.

Ahead, under a beautiful grove of newly sprouting nose hairs, a fully-grown parent germ was in the process of dividing into two kid germs.

'Ooomph,' grunted the parent germ. 'My poor back.'

Aristotle never got tired of watching the miracle of birth. The way a parent germ started to bulge at each end. The way all its insides trickled into one bulge or the other until the parent finally split in half, leaving two identical kids and a couple of faint last words.

'Be good.'

Watching this always made Aristotle think of his own parent, who had turned into him and Blob, and who of course he'd never met.

Which was sad.

Because, Aristotle sometimes thought, perhaps my parent was an odd germ out too. Perhaps my parent could have explained to me why I'm so different from Blob and all the other germs.

Aristotle made himself stop thinking about this now.

He had something much more urgent to do. As he and Blob and their military escort got closer to the two new kid germs, he called out to them.

'Hello.'

If he could make friends with them, and show the authorities that other kids liked having fun too, perhaps, just perhaps, the authorities would let him and Blob stay in the nostril.

'Do you like piggybacks?' said Aristotle to the two new kids.

'No,' said one of the kids.

'And what's more,' said the other kid, 'they're illegal under the terms of the Piggyback Prohibition Act.'

Aristotle sighed.

It was a wonderful thing that kids were born identical replicas of their parent, but it did mean they weren't much fun.

'OK,' he said, talking quickly because the soldiers were prodding him to keep him moving. 'Let's forget piggybacks. Let's play doctors and nurses. It's very popular among humans and flu viruses. They pretend to diagnose each other's medical problems, then have lots of fun pretending to cure them.'

'That's silly,' said one of the kids, trotting along beside Aristotle and Blob. 'Anyway, you're both banished.'

'So banished,' said the other.

'It's a travesty of justice,' moaned Blob. 'I'm innocent.'

'You've only got yourselves to blame,' said the first kid. 'Silly behaviour gets nose cells over-excited and you know what that results in.'

Aristotle didn't. He'd heard rumours, but he didn't believe them.

'Colds,' said the kids, stopping and shuddering. 'Blocked noses. Sneezes.'

Aristotle shuddered too. He'd heard of sneezes.

The most powerful and destructive weather condition known to germs, that's what a sneeze was. But he was pretty sure sneezes weren't caused by piggybacks or birthday cakes.

'Do you like birthday cakes?' Aristotle called back to the kids hopefully.

'Aristotle,' said Blob. 'Shut up.'

There was one more glimmer of hope.

On the way to the nostril exit, the soldiers marched Aristotle and Blob past a dust-sorting depot.

It was a dust-sorting depot Aristotle recognised. Teams of microbes were busily sorting the chunks of dust that flew into the nostril each time the human took a breath. Some of the microbes looked familiar.

'Hi Ralph,' called Aristotle through the fence. 'Hi Fernandez. Hi Preston. Hi Gavin.'

A square-shaped yellow microbe with blue arms and legs heaved a chunk of talcum powder onto a pile of biscuit dust and waved delightedly.

'Hey, Aristotle,' he yelled. 'Good to see you. Have you come to hear more stories about the outside world?'

A triangular purple microbe with several green snouts dropped a lump of playground dust onto a heap of pizza particles, nudged the yellow microbe and pointed to Aristotle's military escort.

'Looks like the poor kid's gunna find out about

the outside world for himself,' said the purple microbe.

The yellow microbe went concerned-shaped. So did a fuzzy orange microbe and a spiral pink one.

Aristotle turned to the platoon commander, who was still prodding him in the back with a spear trying to keep him moving.

'Sir,' said Aristotle. 'Permission to suggest a really good idea, sir.'

The platoon commander signalled to the military escort to stop.

'Quickly,' he barked at Aristotle.

'Well,' said Aristotle, pointing to himself and Blob, and then at Ralph, Fernandez, Preston and Gavin. 'You could swap us for them.'

The platoon commander frowned. Aristotle could see he was struggling to understand.

'These visitors would love to be banished,' explained Aristotle. 'They're only in the nostril by accident because they got breathed in. Send them away and leave me and Blob here. We're really good dust sorters.'

Blob, who'd been staring miserably at the ground, looked startled.

'But I don't know anything about . . .' he started to say.

Aristotle shut him up with a fierce look.

I do, the look said. *I learned heaps about dust-sorting*, the look said, *all those times I snuck out of school to come and talk to these blokes. I even know the tricks they use to pay the authorities back for keeping them prisoner*, the look said.

Blob frowned, puzzled.

Aristotle realised it was too much information for one look.

'I'll sort the dust,' he said to Blob. 'You count it.'

'Not a chance,' snapped the platoon commander. 'My orders are to escort you two out of the nostril. Move.'

Aristotle sagged into a disappointed shape. As he and Blob and the soldiers headed off again, he could see that Ralph, Fernandez, Preston and Gavin were looking pretty disappointed too.

'Stop dawdling,' barked the platoon commander, prodding Aristotle in the back.

'I reckon it's the tragic state of education today, sir,' said one of the soldiers, prodding Aristotle in the back too. 'That's what creates delinquents like this pair.'

Aristotle didn't agree. OK, the classrooms at his school were mostly temporary structures made from dead brain cells, and they got a bit crowded with fifty thousand students in each class. But it wasn't a bad school. And the teachers were brilliant.

He'd miss them.

Aristotle's thoughts were interrupted by more shouting behind him.

He turned round.

Back in the dust-sorting compound, Ralph, Fernandez, Preston and Gavin were waving.

'Thanks for trying,' they yelled.

Aristotle waved back and smiled sadly. In the distance he heard one of the dust-sorting supervisors asking Fernandez what type of dust a chunk of blowfly poo was.

'This?' replied Fernandez, going innocent-shaped. 'This is a pizza particle. Very good eating.'

'Delicious,' said Ralph.

Aristotle heard Preston and Gavin snort as they struggled not to go grin-shaped.

What Aristotle didn't hear at any stage, as the soldiers marched him and Blob towards the nostril exit, was Blob saying anything even a tiny bit like 'thanks for trying'.

The military escort left them at the nostril exit.

Aristotle, peering out at the hazy brightness, felt anxiety churn inside him. He and Blob were about to go where no germ had ever been before. Where even the armed nostril defence force soldiers obviously didn't want to go.

Outside the nostril.

What if Ralph and the others were wrong about the outside world being a fun place? Aristotle had always enjoyed chatting with them, but he'd had a bit of a feeling that they didn't always tell the truth.

Aristotle could see that Blob was as worried as he was.

And even more miserable.

'I'm really sorry, Blob,' said Aristotle. 'It's my fault you're here and I'm going to make it up to you.'

'Thanks,' said Blob, glum-shaped. 'Is that before or after I pass through the digestive system of an armpit-dwelling microbe?'

Aristotle forced himself to go confident-shaped. The effort made his insides hurt.

'We'll be OK, Blob,' he said. 'I promise.'

'Good,' said Blob. 'Is that before or after the nostril defence force turn us into kebabs?'

The platoon commander was waving his spear and signalling for them to leave immediately. Aristotle took a nervous step forward, then stopped for one last look back at the nostril.

'You're blocking the exit,' said Blob. 'Which is in direct contravention of the Nostril Exit Act.'

'What Nostril Exit Act?' said Aristotle.

'The others are voting on it now,' said Blob. 'Along with the No Fond Memories Of Aristotle Act.'

Aristotle sighed and stepped into the outside world.

4

At first the outside world wasn't too bad, except for the painful brightness everywhere.

'The human must have its desk lamp on,' said Aristotle, dazzled.

Blob looked puzzled as well as dazzled. Aristotle explained about the slightly-toasted book microbe who'd been breathed into the nostril once and had told him ruefully about the desk lamp.

'There are worse things than being toasted,' muttered Blob, going scowl-shaped. 'Being banished, for example.'

Aristotle decided to take advantage of the general brightness and look on the bright side. So far things were going well. They'd been travelling for a while and they hadn't been attacked once. And the landscape outside the nostril seemed quite pleasant. It was flat and covered with a forest of slender pale hairs that waved gently in the breeze.

'I wonder what this place is called?' said Aristotle.

'Let me guess,' said Blob. 'Blob's Curse National Park? Dead Blob Gully?'

Aristotle looked sadly at his brother. Poor Blob wasn't cheering up as fast as he'd hoped.

'Come on,' said Aristotle. 'I've got a plan.'

'Oh good,' said Blob, going sarcasm-shaped. 'I'm in the mood for bouncing up and down on something like I'm an idiot. Or were you thinking of making another cake?'

'No,' said Aristotle, struggling to stay calm. 'I'm planning to find us somewhere good to live.'

'There's only one good place,' said Blob. 'The nostril. Count it, one. Everywhere else is horrible. The big toes, the tummies, that bottom flap thing, all horrible. All full of cruel vicious mutant microbes. You've heard the stories. Hordes of protoplasm-thirsty barbarians. They live without rules, laws or reliable statistics. They torture each other for fun. They kill each other for sport. Their whole lifestyle is incredibly untidy.'

Aristotle slumped into a doubt-shape.

What if Blob was right? He'd heard the stories millions of times. It was why the nose germs were always making new laws. So they wouldn't end up bad germs like the ones in the stories.

'I'm sure it's not that awful out here,' said Aristotle. 'Ralph and the others are from outside the nostril and they're really nice.'

'They're idiots,' said Blob, going scorn-shaped. 'Their think molecules are scrambled from being in too many high winds. What was it they told you recently? Humans have got breakfast cereal that makes noise? How mental is that?'

Aristotle had to agree it did sound pretty mental.

'But I still reckon this part of the human looks OK,' he said.

A gloomy voice joined their conversation.

'Don't be fooled by what it looks like.'

Aristotle looked around. And saw, high up on one of the skin hairs, tucked into a split end, a gloomy-looking amoeba.

'This is dangerous territory,' said the amoeba. 'I'd be running away from here if I had legs.'

'Why?' asked Aristotle anxiously.

He could see that Blob was looking pretty anxious too.

'Haven't you heard the old song?' said the amoeba.

Aristotle shook his top bits.

The amoeba swelled his jelly sac and started singing.

North of the lip,
South of the nose,
Here's a good tip,
This is the part of the human face where no single-celled organism with any common sense or basic regard for his own safety ever goes.'

Aristotle shuddered, partly from fear and partly because the amoeba was a very bad singer.

'What's the next verse?' Blob asked the amoeba.

The amoeba didn't reply. Instead it slid off the face hair and plopped onto the ground at their feet, dead.

Aristotle looked around fearfully.

No sign of any cruel vicious mutant microbes. In the distance, through the forest, he could just make out a dark hill towering above the face hairs.

'Let's get out of here,' said Blob, also looking around fearfully.

Aristotle pointed to the hill. 'If we climb up there,' he said, 'we'll be able to see further. Check out the surrounding district. Spot any dangers. Locate a good area to live. Perhaps with bungy-jumping facilities.'

'Good plan,' said Blob. 'Apart from that stupid last bit.'

They hurried on through the face-hair forest. The closer they got to the hill, the bigger and darker it became.

Aristotle wasn't concerned.

What did concern him was something he was noticing about this whole district. He could tell that Blob was noticing it too.

'The amoeba was right,' Blob was muttering. 'Out of tune, but right.'

At first glance the district had pretty much everything you'd imagine on a human face.

Graceful stands of face hair.

Skin flakes billowing into drifts.

Wind-blown eddies of dust and grit.

Only one thing was missing.

Other germs.

'Maybe all the germs around here got old and retired,' puffed Aristotle as he and Blob scrambled up the side of the hill. 'Moved into an old germs' home.'

'What are you talking about?' panted Blob, scorn-shaped again. 'Germs don't retire when they get old. The Retirement Prohibition Act forbids it. We become parents. You know that.'

If Aristotle had any legs to spare from climbing, he would have kicked himself.

'Sorry,' he said. 'I wasn't thinking.'

'Try to concentrate,' grumbled Blob. 'If we're going to get out of this disaster you've got us into, we have to think clearly.'

'Sorry,' said Aristotle.

Blob stopped scrambling and stared suspiciously at the dark hillside they were both standing on.

'Wait a second,' he said. 'What if this hill is cursed? A dark evil curse that kills every germ that comes within half a millimetre of it. Which is why all the local germs stay away.'

Aristotle sighed.

Blob went panic-shaped and started clutching himself all over.

'The curse has got me,' he wailed. 'Look, I've got twitches. And itchy bits. I'm dying.'

'Blob,' said Aristotle quietly. 'This is a mole.

Remember the tiny moles in the nostril? This is a big one.'

Blob stared around at the dark hillside.

Aristotle waited for him to calm down.

'Let's have a little rest,' said Aristotle.

Gently he pushed Blob down onto the bumpy hillside. Then he lay down himself so he and Blob were end to end, feet touching. The exact position they'd been in when their parent had first split in two and they were born.

'That's better,' murmured Aristotle.

He liked doing this. Sometimes, when Blob got fearful and anxious, regulations and laws and counting things weren't enough. That's when Blob needed to pretend he still had a parent.

This time, though, Blob didn't seem to be enjoying it.

'Can we go now?' said Blob.

'Try to stop wriggling,' said Aristotle. 'You'll feel better if you relax.'

'I can't relax,' grumbled Blob. 'This hillside's too uncomfortable. I only like doing this at home. Can we go now?'

'OK,' said Aristotle sadly.

After their very little rest, Aristotle and Blob continued climbing.

The higher they climbed, the more hopeful Aristotle felt about what they'd see in the distance when they got to the top.

Magical lands.

With heaps of sporting equipment.

And birthday party places.

And maybe even hang-gliding places.

Then Aristotle realised something.

Of course, he thought, that's probably where all the local germs are. Off having fun. That's what the amoeba meant about this being a dangerous place. Everyone enjoys themselves so much they're always in danger of forgetting the time.

Aristotle didn't say anything to Blob. He was worried that Blob probably wouldn't agree and might injure himself by trying to go scorn-shaped and scowl-shaped and sarcasm-shaped all at once.

At last they reached the top of the mole.

The view was stunning.

'Wow,' yelled Blob. 'Look at that. You can see our nostril.'

Aristotle looked.

Blob was right. They were up above the forest now. In front of them in the distance was the entire vast nostril entrance.

Aristotle gazed at it and tried not to go sad-shaped. Would he ever see his home and friends again? Probably not.

Oh well, he thought. At least Blob's not taking it all so badly any more.

'Incredible,' Blob was saying, so amazed-shaped his arms were flapping. 'Isn't that the most amazing sight you've ever seen?'

Aristotle agreed it was. Until he turned round and looked in the other direction.

Then he saw a sight that amazed him so much he almost fainted.

'Blob,' he whispered. 'Look.'

Blob didn't turn round.

'Hang on,' said Blob. 'I think I can see some of the germs in the nostril. They look like they're having a meeting. Probably to pass the Aristotle Banishment Bill. Yes, they're voting now. One vote . . . two votes . . . three . . .'

'Blob,' screamed Aristotle.

Blob turned round.

And went so stunned-shaped he looked like he'd been flattened by a large chunk of flying nightie fluff.

Aristotle had never been more stunned-shaped himself. He couldn't believe what he was seeing. It was like something from a dream or a legend or the confused thoughts you have when a flying chunk of talcum powder whacks you in the top bits.

But here it was, in real life, towering majestically next to the nostril he and Blob had just been banished from.

Incredible.

Unbelievable.

Another nostril.

5

Aristotle had never trotted halfway down a mole so quickly. Or tripped and rolled the rest of the way so fast.

He had never scrambled through a face-hair forest so frantically.

And now he was experiencing another first. Hiding behind a dune of toast crumbs, gazing up at . . .

Incredible.

'Incredible,' panted Blob, squeaky with amazement. 'It's another nostril.'

It certainly was.

To make absolutely sure he wasn't having a squiz molecule meltdown, Aristotle peered across at the old nostril, then back at this one, then at the old one, then back at this one again. The old nostril was some distance away, at the other side of a vast skin cliff, but it was definitely there.

Which meant a grand total of . . .

'Two nostrils,' squeaked Blob. 'The human's got two nostrils.'

Aristotle struggled to take this in.

'I don't get it,' said Blob. 'Why would anyone need a second nostril? Particularly when their first one is operating in a very orderly and efficient manner with two hundred and thirty-three thousand six hundred and forty-seven laws, bills, acts, rules, regulations and reminder notices.'

Aristotle's thoughts were spinning.

'Perhaps,' he said, 'since we left, our nostril got old and became a parent?'

Blob gave him a look.

Aristotle could see Blob didn't think this was very likely. He didn't think it was very likely himself now his think molecules were calming down.

'If a human can have three tummies and ten big toes,' said Aristotle, 'I guess it can have two nostrils.'

'We've got to get back and tell the others,' said Blob. 'So they can start passing new laws. For example the Nostril Exit Act will have to become the Nostrils Exit Act. We'll need thousands of meetings. Come on.'

Blob grabbed Aristotle and tried to pull him away from the new nostril. Aristotle pulled harder and dragged Blob back down behind the toast crumbs.

'We can't go back,' said Aristotle. 'We're banished, remember?'

'Don't worry,' said Blob. 'They'll let us in when they hear our news. They'll probably pardon us. I reckon there's an eighty-five percent chance we'll be heroes.'

Aristotle thought about how much the chief judge didn't like him. He went frown-shaped to show Blob he didn't think being unbanished was very likely.

'What if they hate our news?' said Aristotle. 'What if they prefer being an only nostril? What if they banish us for a second time, this time with spears in our top bits?'

He peered round the pile of crumbs into the new nostril.

It was a bit too far away to be certain, but the new nostril looked pretty much like the old one. The shape was exactly the same. And Aristotle could see familiar nose-hair highways criss-crossing the vast internal spaces. Plus he was pretty sure he could make out dust-sorting depots and schools and mucus-mines, all looking very much like the ones at home.

Or rather, thought Aristotle sadly, what used to be home.

'Stop that,' said Blob. 'If you're thinking what I think you're thinking, about going closer for a better look, stop thinking it.'

'I'm going closer for a better look,' said Aristotle.

Before Blob could grab him, Aristotle ducked out from behind the pile of crumbs. He trotted towards the nostril entrance, flattening his body and folding it forward to keep a low profile. He flung himself down behind a fallen face hair and gazed up into the new nostril.

This was better. He could see more clearly now. Yes.

Nose germs, millions of them.

From this distance they looked pretty much like the nose germs at home. They didn't seem to have any strange features, like legs at the top and arms at the bottom. There was one difference, though.

I reckon, thought Aristotle, these germs look happier.

He wasn't close enough to be sure but he didn't think he could see any meetings. These germs seemed to be just wandering around. Probably playing and enjoying themselves and giving each other birthday cakes.

'Don't go any closer, you idiot,' panted a grumpy voice.

It was Blob, flopping down next to him behind the fallen face hair.

'They're nose germs,' said Aristotle excitedly. 'Like us. If we ask nicely, they'll probably let us live with them. It'll be just like at home, but hopefully with less rules and regulations.'

'They might look like us,' said Blob. 'That doesn't mean they are like us. They could be anything. Killers. Criminals. Mutants. Messy eaters. I will not live with messy eaters.'

Aristotle squinted into the new nostril again.

He had to admit he couldn't be certain that these nose germs were exactly like him and Blob, but it would be easy to check.

'They could be cannibals,' said Blob gloomily. 'That would explain why there aren't any germs out here. They've eaten them all.'

Aristotle sighed.

Blob was still panting hard, the fluid wheezing around inside his body. Aristotle worried sometimes that Blob wasn't very fit. It was hard to be fit when you spent all your time at meetings counting votes and never giving other germs piggybacks or going on trampolines. Unfit germs had less energy, and Aristotle often noticed how in Blob's case having less energy meant being gloomy more often.

'I'm going closer,' said Aristotle. 'Just for a peek.'

'No,' said Blob. 'I won't let you. They might have anti-peeking laws.'

Aristotle gave Blob a stern look. Sometimes you had to be strict with your brother, even though he was a twin and had the same voting rights as you. Particularly when it was your fault he'd been banished and it was your responsibility to find him a new home with friendly nose germs and a nice school.

'Stay here,' said Aristotle. 'Keep out of sight. Then, if anything happens to me, you can go and get help.'

Blob went panic-shaped.

'Not that it will,' said Aristotle quickly.

Blob stayed panic-shaped.

Aristotle rolled out from behind the skin hair log. He lay flat on his front and slithered over the rubble of toast crumbs and insect dandruff towards the entrance to the new nostril.

Behind him, faintly, he could hear Blob counting.

For a brief moment Aristotle thought Blob had spotted some nostril defence force guards coming out of the new nostril and was counting them.

Aristotle squinted at the nostril entrance.

He couldn't see any guards.

Aristotle smiled. Blob must just be counting his insides. Whenever Blob got really anxious he tried to calm himself down by counting his own internal organs and other bits and pieces.

Silly old Blob, thought Aristotle fondly. Always worrying. I should have explained to him that we don't have to worry about the nostril defence force here because we're nose germs just like them and we come in peace.

Aristotle was still smiling fondly when he reached the nostril rim.

He stopped and peered around.

Look at that, he said to himself. This nostril's defence force border post is deserted. The germs in this nostril are certainly more relaxed and trusting than the ones at home.

Aristotle crept down the slope towards the nostril floor, where a game of soccer was underway.

He'd heard about soccer from Ralph and the others. Round ball, eleven thousand a side.

It looked fun.

Then Aristotle saw something that made him go completely grin-shaped. Birthday decorations, festooned around the entrance-ramps to several nose hairs.

Yes, he thought happily. This is my kind of nostril.

Suddenly a voice barked out behind him.

'Stay where you are, sunshine. Don't move or we'll have to get rough.'

Aristotle turned round. Advancing towards him, spears at the ready, were several nostril defence force soldiers, just like the ones at home except fiercer and with birthday decorations tucked under some of their arms.

Aristotle started to wonder if this was the best time to be introducing himself and discussing living arrangements and school timetables.

'You're nicked, sunshine,' said one of the soldiers, grabbing Aristotle with a powerful grip.

The other soldiers grabbed Aristotle with equally strong arms. And, in a couple of cases, legs.

'You're coming with us,' said the first soldier.

They started dragging Aristotle into the new nostril.

Aristotle managed one quick peek over the rim.

Blob was staring out from behind the log, even more panic-shaped than before.

Then Aristotle couldn't see him any more.

'Be careful,' gasped Aristotle.

He was saying it to Blob, begging him to stay safe and out of sight. But he soon said it again, to the soldiers. They were being very rough, gripping his arms very tightly as they dragged him across the nostril floor, not caring one bit that most of his arms felt like they were coming out of their sockets.

Suddenly Aristotle wished he'd listened to Blob.

It looked as if Blob was right. These nose germs were thugs and could easily be murderers.

Cannibals, even.

I'm about to find out, thought Aristotle miserably.

'Help,' he said.

This time he was saying it just to Blob.

6

'Another nostril?'

The clerk of the court doubled over with mirth and thumped a pile of ancient legal documents. Bits of skin-flake parchment flew everywhere.

'Another nostril,' he chortled. 'That's a good one.'

Blob sighed.

When he'd calculated there was an eighty-five percent chance the authorities at home would think he was a hero, he'd completely forgotten this meant there was also a fifteen percent chance they'd laugh themselves silly.

The clerk of the court went nostril-shaped and danced around his office.

'Look at me,' he said. 'I'm another nostril.'

Blob felt himself going indignant-shaped.

He could hardly believe this was the same clerk of the court who'd been so officious helping get him and Aristotle banished.

The nostril defence force guards who had brought Blob in from the nostril rim were all laughing as well now.

'Listen,' said Blob. 'It's true. There is definitely a second nostril. I counted it myself.'

The clerk of the court stopped dancing and stepped very close to Blob. Suddenly he was more serious than Blob had ever seen him in all of Aristotle's many trials.

'Did your brother put you up to this?' he said.

'Put me up to what?' said Blob.

'Coming here,' said the clerk. 'With this ridiculous claim about another nostril next door. Is this his idea of revenge, sending you here with a story to make us all look stupid?'

Blob didn't understand. It didn't add up.

'Why would a second nostril make you look stupid?' he asked.

'Because,' said the supreme commander of the nostril defence force, striding into the room and standing close to Blob too, 'we're in charge of nostril security. If there's another nostril, we have a duty to notice it. But there isn't, so we haven't.'

'Exactly,' said the clerk of the court.

'How could you have noticed it?' said Blob. 'You never leave this nostril. None of us do. Ever. Unless we're banished.'

The supreme commander and the clerk of the court looked at each other and thought about this.

'He's got a point,' said the clerk.

'Blimey,' said one of the soldiers. 'So there could be another nostril?'

All the germs in the office went pale, except for Blob, who was already pale.

Blob was feeling very stressed. He had so many anxious questions buzzing round inside him that he'd lost count of them. Which made him feel twice as anxious.

One, he said to himself, do they think I'm a hero or not? Two, will they let me stay? Three, what about the maths homework I've missed? Four, will Aristotle be OK? Those soldiers who grabbed him in the other nostril didn't look very friendly. And they were very rough. Poop, was that five or six?

Blob realised the clerk of the court was speaking to him again.

'Young germ,' the clerk was saying. 'If I take you to tell your story to the chief judge, do you know what will happen to you if your story isn't true?'

Blob felt a surge of nervousness and relief all at once.

That was definitely question number seven.

'I'll be banished again?' he said.

'Worse,' said the clerk of the court. 'Much worse.'

'Another nostril?'

The chief judge looked as though his outside layer was going to pop.

I hope not, thought Blob.

He started to calculate how long it would take

to clean up the chief judge's protoplasm if it was splattered all around the judge's chamber, and how many germs would be required, and how many . . .

'Are you listening to me?' roared the judge.

Blob went apology-shaped.

'Sorry,' he squeaked.

'I was asking you,' said the judge, 'whether this is your brother's idea of revenge, sending you here with this story to make us all look stupid.'

'We don't think it is,' said the clerk of the court. 'We think the other nostril might be real.'

'But it's not our fault,' said the supreme commander of the nostril defence force.

'We've never even been out of the nostril,' said one of the soldiers.

'I'm asking *him*,' roared the judge.

Blob had started calculating how long a rescue party would take to get to the other nostril and rescue Aristotle before the murderous thugs there started doing horrible things. Not that Aristotle deserved it. Irresponsible, that's what he was. And sloppy. And careless. And silly.

Blob began running through the other eighty-three personal faults of Aristotle's that he'd thought of while he was waiting to see the chief judge.

Then he realised the chief judge was yelling at him again.

'Sorry,' said Blob.

'Young germ,' growled the chief judge. 'If I take you to tell your story to the prime minister, do you know what will happen to you if your story isn't true?'

Blob thought for a moment.

'You'll take me back to the other nostril?' he said. 'And let the germs there eat me?'

The chief judge stared at Blob.

Poor thing, thought Blob. He doesn't look well.

'Another nostril?'

The prime minister stared at Blob, and Blob could see the prime minister's think molecules actually whizzing around inside him.

He decided not to count them. He'd never been this close to a prime minister before and he wasn't sure if counting a prime minister's inside bits was legal.

'This other nostril,' said the prime minister. 'Is it bigger than ours?'

Blob gulped. He'd never been asked a question by a prime minister before either. Apart from the little one a bit earlier, but that didn't really count.

It was a big responsibility.

'Um ... I think it's about the same size,' said Blob. 'Give or take two percent. Or three percent. Two point five. Two point seven five. I could go and measure it.'

The other government ministers in the government meeting room looked at each other.

'I'm sure it's not as beautiful,' said the minister for the environment.

'Or as well-defended,' said the minister for defence.

'Or as well-organised,' said the minister for government committees.

'How do you know?' said the prime minister, looking hard at the other ministers. 'Have you all seen it too?'

The ministers all looked at the floor and admitted they hadn't.

The room fell silent, except for the gentle trickle of blood running through the veins and capillaries in the walls.

After a while, Blob realised all the government ministers were looking at him.

He felt embarrassed.

They were very important ministers.

In the government.

Why were they looking at him?

Then he realised why. They were expecting him, the only germ there who'd seen the other nostril, to be patriotic and stand up for the nostril of his birth.

'Um . . .' said Blob. 'The germs next door are very silly. For example, they play soccer. And they leave birthday decorations lying around their highway entrance ramps.'

The ministers looked relieved.

'And they're not as friendly as us,' added Blob.

'I think we should kill them all,' said the minister for defence.

Blob gulped again. He hoped the minister was joking. He was ninety-nine percent sure the minister was.

Ninety-two percent.

Eighty percent.

Sixty-six.

'These are criminals,' said the minister for defence. 'They've kidnapped one of our citizens.'

Blob realised the minister for defence wasn't joking. He looked at the prime minister, hoping the prime minister had a different plan. One that didn't involve Aristotle accidentally being killed in an orgy of violence.

The prime minister was gazing out over his estate, staring thoughtfully at the distant mucus fountains and the colourful viruses in their cages.

Blob could see the prime minister's think molecules whizzing around again. They were very big think molecules for a germ, which was probably why he was prime minister.

There was more silence, except for the gurgling walls.

Suddenly the prime minister turned and spoke directly to Blob.

'I'm not completely convinced there is another nostril,' he said. 'Please don't feel offended, Blab, but you are the brother of a very silly germ.'

'Blob,' said Blob. 'It's Blob.'

'What we need,' said the prime minister, 'is an intelligence report. I'm going to send a team of our very best intelligence agents to locate this other nostril and, if it exists, to report on any threat it might pose to our nostril security.'

Blob thought about this.

So far the prime minister hadn't mentioned anything about rescuing Aristotle. Blob wondered if he could form a rescue mission himself. He was pretty well connected. He knew over three million germs by name.

'You'll go with them,' said the prime minister to Blob. 'To show them the way.'

'We'll get your brother out of there,' said the minister for defence.

Blob felt weak with relief.

'And when we've finished our mission,' said Blob, 'will me and Aristotle be allowed to come back home, you know, now we've proved we're responsible citizens and sensible individuals and very good explorers?'

The prime minister looked at Blob and slowly shook his top bits.

Even before he added, 'Don't be silly, you're banished,' Blob had gone miserable-shaped.

7

Inside the other nostril, Aristotle was miserable-shaped, too.

'Come on, sunshine,' said the nostril defence force sergeant, pushing Aristotle in the back. 'Get a move on.'

Aristotle forced his tired legs to trot a bit faster.

He'd been getting a move on for what seemed like ages now. He and the soldiers escorting him were deep inside the evil nostril.

'Is it much further?' asked Aristotle.

The further it was, the more chances he might have to escape before they got to the jail or cannibal restaurant or wherever they were taking him.

The soldiers all went chortle-shaped.

Aristotle didn't get it.

What was funny about asking if it was much further?

'Excitement of long-distance travel dulled your memory, has it?' said one of the soldiers.

The others stayed chortle-shaped.

Aristotle went puzzled-shaped. Since he'd been in this other nostril, just about everything he'd seen and heard had puzzled him.

The germs here, for example. OK, they were obviously nasty pieces of work if these rough and thuggish nostril defence force goons were anything to go by. But on the outside they all looked totally normal to Aristotle.

Just like the germs at home.

As he squinted around the nostril and watched the locals at school and work and soccer practice and putting up birthday decorations, he couldn't see a single sign of evil.

No eating each other.

No murdering each other.

Not even bursting each other's balloons.

Maybe they know how to hide the bad stuff, thought Aristotle. Maybe that's part of their evil ways.

'Looking more familiar, sunshine?' said one of the soldiers, giving Aristotle another push.

Why would I be looking more familiar? thought Aristotle.

Being hard to understand was probably part of their evil ways too.

He wished the soldiers would stop calling him sunshine. Sunshine was the glowing golden stuff that lit up the nostril at home when the human was at the beach. At the moment Aristotle didn't feel glowing or golden.

'Here we are,' said one of the soldiers.

Aristotle looked around.

And went surprised-shaped.

They'd arrived at a dust-sorting depot. It looked exactly like the dust-sorting depots at home. Same big piles of talcum powder and toast crumbs. Same supervisors complaining about sock fluff in the playground dust. Same teams of exotic blow-in microbes purposely putting bits of kitty litter in with the pizza particles.

Aristotle felt a pang of homesickness. The exotic visitors working in this dust-sorting depot looked just as friendly as Ralph, Fernandez, Preston and Gavin.

Then he remembered there was an important difference between this dust-sorting depot and the ones at home.

At home, thought Aristotle grimly, innocent germs aren't taken to dust-sorting depots to be killed and eaten.

'OK, sunshine,' said the sergeant. 'Ready to go back to work?'

Aristotle stared at the sergeant.

He wasn't sure if he'd heard right.

The sergeant chuckled.

'Wondering how we know you work here, eh?'

The sergeant reached over and tapped Aristotle on the back.

'Not too good at catching dust chunks,' he said. 'You've got dust dents all over your back.'

Aristotle's think molecules started whizzing.

The dents must be from when he was prodded by all those spears while he was being banished. His outer membrane had been so tense ever since, the dents hadn't had a chance to fade.

This is incredible, thought Aristotle as he struggled not to show how incredible he thought it was.

The soldiers think I work here.

They think I'm from this nostril.

'Welcome home,' said the sergeant. 'We hope you enjoyed your little adventure.'

Aristotle stared at the soldiers.

Suddenly they didn't seem quite so rough and thuggish after all.

Aristotle started to picture a whole new wonderful future, living here in this nostril where the germs were actually quite friendly once you got to know them. Working as a dust-sorter. Joining a soccer team. Developing birthday decoration skills. When Blob got back with a rescue party, if they asked nicely, he could probably live here too.

'Thank you,' said Aristotle to the soldiers. 'Thank you very much.'

Another thought hit him, and he went grin-shaped. In all the time he'd been in this nostril, he hadn't seen the germs here hold a single meeting or pass a single law, rule or regulation.

This is my kind of place, thought Aristotle happily.

'Just before you go back to work,' said the sergeant, 'there is the little matter of the charges.'

'Charges?' said Aristotle, puzzled. 'You mean I have to pay for being brought here?'

'Very wry and humorous,' said the sergeant. 'No, sunshine, I mean the criminal charges that you will, in due course, be charged with.'

Aristotle wasn't grin-shaped any more.

'As I'm sure you know,' continued the sergeant, 'committing a little stroll out of the nostril is a criminal offence, as well as being extremely dangerous and very silly. I refer you to section eleven of the Travel Prohibition Act, section thirty-nine of the Stay At Home Act, paragraph three of the Germ Protection Ordinance, article nine in the Nostril Bill Of Rights And Other Forbidden Stuff, and all six hundred and fourteen of the Fun Limitation And Discouragement (Except For Soccer) Regulations.'

Aristotle went sag-shaped.

He tried to speak, but his chat molecules were as numb as the rest of him.

Come on, he begged his chat molecules, this is urgent.

He had to explain.

He had to tell the soldiers there'd been a mistake, that he wasn't from this nostril.

'Is there something you want to say?' asked the sergeant. 'Before I go back to the office and start processing the charges?'

'Yes,' said Aristotle, relieved he could finally get some words out. 'There is. Quite a lot, actually.'

'Another nostril?'

The king stared at Aristotle.

Aristotle waited for the king to go stunned-shaped.

All the other nose germs in the vast palace throne room already had. Aristotle had himself, just from seeing the royal palace. It was the most magnificent building he'd ever been in that was constructed entirely from bits of tissues.

The king didn't go stunned-shaped.

Aristotle had never met a king before, so he didn't know whether to be surprised or not. He decided kings were probably trained to stay king-shaped at all times.

'Has anyone else seen this other nostril?' demanded the king.

'My brother Blob,' said Aristotle. 'He used to live there with me. Until we had to leave. Because of the birthday cake.'

The several thousand royal advisers and consultants and other important-looking germs in the room all started muttering to each other and frowning and scratching their outside layers and looking as if they wished they were somewhere else.

Aristotle wasn't sure what was going on.

'All right, calm down,' snapped the king. 'We've been through this already. You forgot my birthday, no big deal. You remembered eventually, the decorations are going up, my birthday banquet is being prepared and I'm sure each of you is planning a very special surprise or gift for me. So please, let's forget about it.'

The royal advisers and consultants all looked ill.

Except one.

'If I may, your majesty,' said a particularly important-looking germ. He was obviously a senior royal adviser. The other advisers stepped back to give him room.

Aristotle couldn't help staring. The senior royal adviser had the most unusual-shaped body he'd ever seen on a germ. It was narrow in the middle with a large bulge at the bottom and another at the top. It looked to Aristotle as if the senior royal adviser had started to become a parent but then changed his mind halfway through.

'Go ahead,' said the king.

'Unfortunately,' said the senior adviser, 'the birthday banquet has been delayed a little, due to a mucus mishap.'

The king frowned.

'A mucus mishap?' he said.

The senior royal adviser looked uncomfortable.

'On the way here,' he said, 'we locked the young germ in a storeroom. Unfortunately he spent the time bouncing up and down on the mucus for your birthday banquet.'

The king glowered at Aristotle.

Aristotle felt himself trembling. He'd never been glowered at by a king before.

'I'm sorry, your majesty,' he said. 'I was just trying to work off some stress.'

'So you bounced up and down on my birthday dinner?' said the king.

'Yes,' said Aristotle quietly. 'Sorry. I can't help myself sometimes. If you want to throw me out of your nostril I won't mind.'

The king gave Aristotle a long look.

'Are all the germs in the other nostril like you?' he said.

Aristotle thought about this.

'Not really,' he said sadly.

The king and the senior royal adviser exchanged a glance. Aristotle had the feeling they didn't believe him.

'He's almost certainly suffering from a tragic delusion,' said the senior royal adviser. 'There almost certainly isn't another nostril. But we can't take any chances. Not if there might be a few million like him next door.'

The king thought about this.

'If a royal scouting party goes with you,' said the king to Aristotle, 'would you be able to show us this other nostril?'

Aristotle paused.

He didn't think the folks at home would mind. And it would be a way of getting out of here and finding Blob.

'OK,' he said.

The palace throne room erupted into a buzz of conversation. Everywhere Aristotle looked, important-looking germs were muttering and whispering to each other and giving him suspicious stares. The senior royal adviser was speaking softly to the king, and they were giving him suspicious stares too.

Oh dear, thought Aristotle. I hope I'm doing the right thing. I hope the folks at home won't mind. If they're not in the mood for visitors, they won't be very pleased with me.

8

As Blob slithered through the face-hair forest, he wasn't very pleased with Aristotle.

This is all your fault, Aristotle, he thought crossly. If you hadn't got us banished and then wandered into that other nostril, I wouldn't have to be scraping my front bits ragged rescuing you.

It was the first time Blob had ever been on an intelligence and rescue mission, and he wasn't enjoying it.

'Go faster,' said the senior intelligence agent.

He prodded Blob in the bottom with an item of very sharp secret-agent equipment that looked like a skin flake but, Bob suspected, could kill you if you didn't obey orders.

'I'm going as fast as I can,' said Blob.

He was.

He could be going faster, but only if the senior intelligence agent dropped this ridiculous idea of the whole lot of them slithering through the face-hair forest on their fronts.

The forest floor was strewn with rubble. Blob's outer layer was ragged with toast-crumb cuts and kitty-litter scrapes.

He glanced back at the three thousand two hundred and fourteen intelligence agents slithering behind him. They didn't seem to be having any trouble. Must be the training.

'Ouch,' grunted Blob as a chunk of something gouged him in the guts.

The disguises weren't helping, either.

'Can I take this off now, please?' said Blob.

'No,' said the senior agent. 'We could encounter hostile forces at any time. We must keep our identities hidden.'

Blob didn't get it. It didn't add up. How was pretending to be tummy germs going to help them?

The bits of bacon and spinach were really uncomfortable on his back, and the smears of Vegemite on his outer membrane were stinging.

As Blob slithered painfully towards the mole hill looming up ahead, he worried about what else might be looming up ahead.

Cannibal germs from the other nostril.

He hoped this wasn't going to turn into one of those rescue missions he'd heard stories about. The ones that exploded into violence with a ninety-six percent chance of germs getting hurt, including the one who's showing the others how to get there.

Not that it matters, thought Blob miserably. Thanks to Aristotle, I'll never get to go home again anyway.

A chunk of something sharp and painful stabbed Blob in a tender spot in his middle. The same spot that used to tingle with pleasure when he went on pimple counting trips with Aristotle to remote parts of their nostril. Way back in their early hours together.

Before he found out his brother was a silly idiot.

In another part of the face-hair forest, Aristotle hoped he wasn't being a silly idiot.

He was worried.

The royal scouting party was worrying him.

For a start, they looked more like commandos. They were all armed with semi-automatic spears, and as they trotted through the face-hair forest towards his and Blob's nostril, they were singing worrying commando songs.

'Excuse me,' panted Aristotle to the commando officer. 'This is a peaceful mission, isn't it?'

Aristotle was putting on a spurt to keep up with the commando officer. His legs were aching. So was his back. The scouting party were all trotting with their bodies flattened and folded forward to keep a low profile. Aristotle had only ever done that for a short trot, not a long trot like this one.

'Very peaceful mission,' replied the commando

officer, scanning the forest ahead with a grim squint. 'Our orders are to peacefully gather intelligence about this other nostril of yours.'

'It's just that the song your men are singing,' said Aristotle, 'seems to be about violence and killing.'

'Oh no,' said the commando officer. 'I don't think so.'

'That chorus they've just finished,' said Aristotle. 'They kept repeating the words *waste the microbes, squish their guts out*.'

'Did they?' said the commando officer.

'Yes,' said Aristotle. 'And *kill ninety-nine percent of all known germs*.'

'Ah, yes,' said the commando officer. 'That's just a training song.'

'A training song?' panted Aristotle.

'They sing it to keep cheerful,' said the officer. 'It's good to keep cheerful on a peaceful mission.'

Aristotle thought about this as he and the royal scouting commando unit started to trot up the mole hill and his legs started to hurt a lot.

Yes, he said to himself doubtfully. Cheerful is good.

He was still worried.

I hope Blob's OK, he thought anxiously. And I hope he stays out of the way when these commandos get to our nostril.

Just in case.

Suddenly Aristotle missed his brother so much it hurt even more than his legs. OK, his brother could be grumpy sometimes. OK, his brother counted things a bit too often. But Aristotle knew, as he struggled up the side of the mole hill, that no amount of grumpy counting could ever make him stop loving Blob.

I hate you, Aristotle, thought Blob as he dragged his aching body up the other side of the mole hill.

By hate, he didn't mean he wished Aristotle any harm. Not like the harm he was suffering as the rubble scraped his tender bits and the senior intelligence agent prodded his other tender bits. Not like the stress he was feeling as the rest of the intelligence agents just over his shoulder muttered about him not knowing the way.

By hate Blob just meant he wished he had another germ as his brother. Any one of the other sixty-three million four hundred and ninety-eight thousand seven hundred and forty-two germs in his nostril would do.

Anyone except Aristotle.

Please.

'Leaping lymphocytes,' gasped the commando officer.

Aristotle watched nervously as the officer and the rest of the royal scouting commando unit had their first view of a nostril that wasn't their own.

'Blimey,' one of the commandos said to the others as they stared, stunned-shaped, at Aristotle's nostril. 'It's true. He's not an idiot after all.'

Aristotle peered at his nostril too, hoping to see Blob.

No sign of him, sadly.

'Atten-shun,' shouted the commando officer.

Aristotle stood to attention. The commandos immediately stopped being stunned and snapped back into regulation commando shapes. But they all still gazed at the nostril.

Suddenly Aristotle realised that he and the commandos weren't alone on the top of the mole hill. Slithering over the ridge on the other side were a large number of germs with human food draped over themselves.

Aristotle stared at them, alarmed but also disgusted.

They must be very messy eaters.

Could they be tummy germs?

They looked more like nose germs in fancy dress.

Now they were staring too, stunned-shaped, at the new nostril. All of them except one, who was peering at Aristotle.

Aristotle peered back.

Was it?

Could it be?

The peering germ took off a scarf of bacon and a hat of spinach, and Aristotle saw that it was.

'Blob,' he yelled.

He started to trot towards his brother. But his way was blocked. The commandos had all stopped staring at Aristotle's nostril and were on full battle alert, facing the fancy-dress germs. The fancy-dress germs, who Aristotle realised must be from home, were doing the same to the commandos.

'Don't attack until I give the order,' shouted the commando officer.

'Ditto,' shouted the senior intelligence agent.

Aristotle trembled in the middle.

This is tragic, he thought. These are all nose germs, all the same underneath their military equipment and bits of bacon, but they just don't know it yet.

He had to do something.

'Excuse me,' he shouted to the commandos and intelligence agents. 'Can I have your attention please?'

He waited until both sides had stopped glowering at each other.

'Hello,' he said. 'I'm Aristotle and this is my brother Blob. Um . . . as you can see, there are two nostrils. That makes us neighbours so we should probably do some introductions and get to know each other. Blob, why don't you start.'

Blob stared at Aristotle and went a weird shape Aristotle didn't recognise.

After a few moments, Aristotle remembered that Blob wasn't very good in big social groups. Counting them, yes. Talking to them, no.

Aristotle was about to do the introductions himself when, to his surprise, Blob started speaking.

'Actually,' said Blob to the assembled military personnel, 'I'm not sure if Aristotle is my brother. I've been thinking about it and I reckon there might have been a mix-up at birth.'

Aristotle stared at Blob, numb with shock.

Then he realised what was happening.

Of course, chuckled Aristotle to himself. It's been an hour since I gave him the cake. It's our birth anniversary. We're eleven. He's playing a birthday joke on me. This is wonderful. Blob's actually playing a joke.

'Happy birthday, Blob,' said Aristotle happily, and gave his brother a big hug.

Blob pulled away.

Some of the commandos and intelligence agents gasped.

'I mean it, Aristotle,' said Blob, miserable-shaped. 'How can me and you be brothers? We're just too different.'

Aristotle struggled to find something to say, something that would end this birthday nightmare and make things all right.

But before he could, there was a terrible rumbling squelching sound.

Aristotle looked around, startled.

And saw a truly horrifying sight.

Surging towards the hilltop from the south was a massive greasy white wave. Aristotle had never seen anything like it. For a few moments he didn't know what it was. Then the commandos and intelligence agents all started yelling in panic.

'Whipped cream.'

Aristotle froze, mesmerised by fear.

Whipped cream. He'd learned about it at school. The deadliest substance known to nose germs. Deadly because its fat content made it so easy for germs to absorb through their membranes, but once they had, the sugar content sent them into shock and spasms and . . .

Aristotle didn't want to think about it.

'Blob,' he yelled.

Commandos and intelligence agents were scrambling in all directions. Aristotle saw Blob knocked spinning onto his back by a burly fleeing commando.

'Blob,' yelled Aristotle again, flinging himself at his brother and trying desperately to drag Blob by the legs across the hilltop away from the thundering white wave.

Aristotle knew they weren't going to make it.

He stared sadly at his brother, and just for a second Blob stared back.

Then the whipped cream hit, and everything went black.

9

What a nice surprise, thought Aristotle. Somebody's made me a birthday cake. What a nice thing to wake up to when you've been unconscious.

Candlelight danced over Aristotle's dazed squiz molecules.

Very bright candlelight.

Was Blob here?

Had Blob made a cake for him?

Aristotle tried to stand up, but he was too weak. Ouch.

That candlelight was much too bright.

'So,' said a voice Aristotle sort of recognised. 'Are you going to be a good germ and tell us everything? Or are we going to have to smell you?'

Aristotle didn't know what the voice meant. The only thing he did know was that the voice wasn't Blob's.

He squinted through the light. All he could see of the germ standing in front of him was a dark outline. It was an outline he'd seen before. A bulge at the top and a bulge at the bottom.

'Where's Blob?' whispered Aristotle.

'Blob?' said the senior royal adviser.

'My brother,' said Aristotle.

'We don't know,' said the senior royal adviser. 'We wish we did, because we'd like to interrogate him too. But sadly we've only got you. So let's start with the whipped cream. When did your government first have the idea of attacking us with it?'

Aristotle went stunned-shaped.

'Attacking you with it?' he said. 'Nobody attacked you with it. Whipped cream is a natural disaster.'

The senior royal adviser stepped closer. He said something to the candles and they went even brighter. Except, Aristotle now realised, they weren't candles. They were big clusters of very bright carbon molecules that had obviously been trained to dazzle a suspect's squiz molecules during questioning.

'Think carefully, young germ,' said the senior royal adviser. 'Our commandos saved you from the whipped cream and brought you back here so you could tell us the truth.'

'Could you turn the lights down a bit, please?' said Aristotle. 'They're hurting me.'

'If I do,' said the senior royal adviser, 'will you tell us everything you know about the whipped cream?'

'Yes,' said Aristotle.

The senior adviser gave another order, and the carbon molecules dimmed.

Aristotle's squiz molecules gradually stopped hurting and he looked around. He was lying on the ground in an aroma processing plant. It looked a bit like one he had gone to once on a school excursion. Smell-centre germs were grabbing aroma molecules as they came floating into the nostril on the wind.

Homesickness stabbed through Aristotle. He wished he was still on the school excursion with Blob.

But he wasn't.

He was in a different nostril, in a different aroma processing plant. One that was full of grim-shaped royal advisers staring at him.

'I should warn you,' said the senior royal adviser, 'that you are in very serious trouble. We know your brother is a high-ranking officer in the armed forces of your nostril. We know he led the vicious and unprovoked whipped cream attack on our commandos. We believe you are a spy who was sent here by your government to lure our defence force into that brutal ambush.'

Aristotle went gobsmacked-shaped so violently he almost split his outer layer.

'It's not true,' he said. 'None of it.'

The senior adviser's two bulges twitched.

Aristotle could see he wasn't happy.

'We thought that might be your answer,' said the senior adviser. 'So we've set up a little test for you.'

Two military germs grabbed Aristotle and dragged him to his feet.

'Let me introduce you to Len,' said the senior adviser.

Standing next to the senior royal adviser, towering over him, was a smell-centre germ quite a bit bigger than the others.

'Hello,' said Aristotle nervously.

'Whipped cream,' said Len, sniffing in Aristotle's direction. 'Bacon and spinach. Vegemite.'

'As you can see,' the senior adviser said to Aristotle, 'Len is a very capable aroma worker. But he has extra skills. He can also smell if someone is lying.'

Len went modest-shaped.

'It's just this talent I've got,' he said. 'If you tell a porky, tiny fear atoms sneak out through your outer membrane and I can smell 'em. The boffins reckon it might be on account of my unusually large nucleus and inflamed . . .'

'Thank you, Len,' interrupted the senior adviser. 'Let's get started.'

Len came over and stood very close to Aristotle.

'Don't mind me,' he said. 'Just pretend I'm not here.'

Aristotle looked up at Len and gave a nervous smile. A smile looked innocent and truthful, he knew that.

And I am innocent, he thought. So all I've got to do is be truthful.

'Why,' said the senior royal adviser, 'does your government want to attack us?'

'They don't,' said Aristotle.

Len frowned, then shrugged.

'He's telling the truth,' he said.

Aristotle saw that the senior royal adviser was frowning too.

'Then why,' said the senior adviser, 'did your government send you to spy on us?'

'They didn't,' said Aristotle.

He was about to explain how he'd been banished, but then he stopped himself. Governments who did banishing might not sound completely friendly, and Aristotle didn't want to make the royal adviser any twitchier than he already was.

'He's telling the truth,' said Len.

The senior adviser was scowling now.

'Tell us everything you know about the whipped cream,' he snapped at Aristotle.

'Um . . .' said Aristotle. He struggled to remember what he'd learned about it at school. 'Whipped cream is a natural disaster that happens when a human takes a bite of a pastry, bun or other dessert that's too big for its mouth and the human starts choking and creates a tragic tidal wave across its top lip and sometimes breathes some up its nose.'

Aristotle shuddered.

Talking about it was bringing back the horror.

Please, he begged silently. Please let Blob have survived it too.

'He's telling the truth,' said Len.

The senior adviser twitched quite a lot.

'I find this hard to believe,' he said tersely. 'Len, are you sure you're not having an off day? What aftershave am I wearing?'

Len looked hurt.

'Three molecules of Old Spice,' he said. 'And one molecule of Imperial Leather and one molecule of Arctic Splash. You really shouldn't mix them.'

'I can't get a regular supply,' muttered the senior adviser.

He turned to Aristotle.

'I'm impressed,' he said. 'Not many get past Len.'

Aristotle felt weak with relief.

'Does that mean I can go now?' he asked.

'I'm afraid not,' said the senior adviser. 'We in this peace and freedom loving nostril have a problem. We find we have a neighbouring nostril that might not be very nice. That might threaten our way of life. We need to find out more about the germs who live there. And you're the only one we've got.'

Aristotle didn't like the sound of this.

'And,' continued the senior adviser, 'because on the outside you don't look any different to us, I'm afraid we're going to have to . . .'

The senior adviser paused with what seemed to Aristotle to be genuine regret.

Aristotle didn't like the sound of that pause. And he also didn't like the look of the germs approaching him now. The ones carrying what appeared to be pieces of scientific equipment.

Some of them horribly sharp-looking.

'I'm afraid,' said the senior adviser, 'we're going to have to take a look inside you.'

10

Blob felt like he'd been picked out of a nostril by a giant finger, rolled into a ball and flicked into a crowd of angry tummy germs.

Well, he was pretty sure he did.

He couldn't be certain because he'd never actually had the experience. But he was ninety-six percent sure that having the experience would leave you feeling as mangled and upset as the experiences he had been having.

Being almost smothered by whipped cream.

Being dragged back to your own nostril and scrubbed in a military hospital till your outer layer nearly peeled off.

Being left alone in a ward minute after minute after minute with nothing to do except think about the germ who might or might not be your brother. How that germ had gone bravely into a strange nostril to try and find somewhere for you both to live. How he'd tried to save you from the whipped cream, even though it might have cost him his own life.

Blob felt very sad having those thoughts about Aristotle. So sad that even counting dead skin cells on the hospital wall hadn't made him feel better.

And then, on top of all that, Blob had been rushed to a secret location, which he now recognised as one of the eleven hundred and ninety-four abandoned mucus mines in the nostril, where the prime minister and fifty-three percent of the government were waiting impatiently for him.

'Young germ,' said the prime minister as soon as Blob's police escort had left. 'I have a very important question for you, and you must tell the truth. Do you understand?'

Blob struggled to concentrate. He couldn't get Aristotle out of his thoughts.

'Do you understand?' repeated the prime minister.

'No,' said Blob. 'Yes. I think so.'

'Good,' said the prime minister. 'Here's the question. Does your brother know any secrets about this nostril, any secrets at all, that would put our freedom at risk if a hostile nostril, any hostile nostril, found out about those secrets?'

Blob tried desperately to understand the question.

It wasn't easy. A lot of very important germs were looking at him. He felt himself starting to panic.

He counted to ten silently to calm himself. He

would have preferred ten thousand, but he could see the prime minister was getting impatient. The prime minister's big lazily-floating molecules were starting to speed up. Blob resisted the temptation to count them.

'We're waiting,' said the prime minister.

'Um . . .' said Blob. 'That's a pretty big question. Thirty-two words. Can I have a little bit more time to think about it?'

The prime minister nodded.

Blob thought hard.

He thought about which answer would be best for Aristotle.

He was ninety-nine percent sure Aristotle would never give away his recipe for fluffy skin-flake icing. But what if he did, and what if a hostile enemy made it with sugar and used it in an attack . . .?

Blob forced the thought away. Mentioning that could get Aristotle into trouble.

'The answer's no,' said Blob.

'No secrets he'd give away,' said the prime minister, 'even if he was being tortured?'

Blob stared blankly at the prime minister.

'Tortured?' he said.

'Tortured,' said the prime minister.

Blob went confused-shaped.

'Who would want to torture Aristotle?' he said. 'That's crazy. He's one of the nicest germs you could meet. Very silly, and I could kill him sometimes, but torture . . .'

Blob was lost for words.

'They are torturing him,' said the prime minister. 'Right now.'

Blob felt like he'd been slapped with a cold cold-germ.

'Why?' he whispered.

'We don't know why,' said the prime minister. 'That's why we're asking you. But we do know that your brother is being held prisoner by those ingermane brutes in the other nostril, and we do know they're torturing him.'

Blob struggled to take this in.

'How do you know?' he asked.

'One of our intelligence agents got in there,' said the prime minister. 'He's just reported back. I'm sorry.'

A piece of dried mucus that Blob had assumed was just one of the many pieces of dried mucus in the old mine now stepped forward and spoke.

'They're using sharp kitchen implements,' said the intelligence agent, loosening his dried mucus suit.

Blob felt himself reeling.

'We've got to do something,' he said, going pleading-shaped. He looked around at the government ministers.

He didn't understand.

Why wouldn't any of them look at him?

'In a few minutes,' said the prime minister, 'we will be doing something. We'll be hitting that evil

76

nostril with the biggest invasion force they've ever seen. We'll be blowing those criminal thugs to oblivion. When we've finished with them, they'll be a bunch of corpses in a human's hanky.'

Blob stared at the prime minister in horror.

'We'll be teaching those evil monsters,' continued the prime minister, 'that you do not kidnap and mistreat innocent germs, and you do not attack citizens of a free and peace-loving nostril with whipped cream.'

'But . . .' said Blob.

'No buts,' said the prime minister. 'Every germ in that nostril will pay the price for their evil ways. When we've finished blasting them, that nostril will be cleansed by the wind of peace and freedom.'

The government ministers clapped and cheered.

'But what if Aristotle's still in there when you attack?' said Blob. 'He could be killed too.'

The cheering ministers didn't hear him. They were still cheering when the police arrived to take Blob back to the military hospital.

Blob allowed himself to be led away.

One desperate thought burned inside his over-scrubbed and Vegemite-tinged outer layer.

I've got to get to Aristotle, Blob said to himself, and warn him.

'Please,' begged Aristotle. 'Stop. I can't take any more.'

'Give him another,' said the senior royal adviser.

'No,' moaned Aristotle.

'It's cake,' said the senior royal adviser. 'You like cake.'

'I'm full,' groaned Aristotle. 'I've had six pieces.'

'It's talcum-powder and playground-dust cake with fluffy skin-flake icing,' said the senior royal adviser. 'You told us it's your favourite.'

'It is,' said Aristotle. 'But I'm stuffed.'

'If you don't eat,' said the senior royal adviser crossly, 'you won't grow up to be a happy healthy germ like me.'

He patted both his bulges.

Aristotle slumped back in the big chair that was carved from a single massive chunk of sawdust. He was so full he felt like a single massive chunk of sawdust himself. He tried not to look at the food that was piled on the huge banquet table in front of him. He also tried not to look at the royal chefs, who were bringing in yet more platters.

Mucus steaks.

Skin cream and burnt toast trifles.

Great haunches of virus.

'Please,' begged Aristotle. 'Enough.'

'He can stop now,' said one of the scientists crouched around Aristotle peering in through his transparent outer membrane. 'We're done.'

Aristotle gave a big sigh of relief.

It was almost as big as the sigh of relief he'd given earlier when he'd realised the scientists weren't planning to cut him open and the germs carrying the sharp-looking equipment were just chefs.

'So?' said the senior adviser to the scientists. 'What are the results? What have you found? Is he different to us, and if so, how?'

Aristotle listened carefully. He was very keen to know the answers to these questions too.

'His digestive system's just the same as ours,' said one of the scientists. 'We've got exact matches on digestive system, body structure, wobbliness of protoplasm, number of arms and legs, and how tickly he is.'

Aristotle shivered at the memory of the tickle test. He never wanted to see sock fluff ever again.

'As far as we can tell,' said the scientist, 'he's exactly the same as us.'

No, Aristotle wanted to yell. I'm not the same as

you. I'm different. I don't like rules and regulations. I don't like counting things. Sometimes I go a bit silly. Come on, you scientists, tell me why.

But he kept quiet.

Calm down, he said to himself. You're a prisoner in a hostile nostril and the germs here are hoping you're the same as them so they won't have to invade your nostril and kill all your friends and your brother. Telling them how different you are would be just a little bit silly.

'Hmmm,' said the senior royal adviser, looking closely at Aristotle. 'So on the physical evidence at least, we're not living next to a nostril full of dangerously ingermane mutants.'

Aristotle wasn't sure exactly what ingermane mutants were, but that didn't stop him trying to reassure the royal adviser.

'Definitely no dangerous ingermane mutants in our nostril,' said Aristotle. 'In fact we have an Ingermane Mutant Control And Regulation Act that makes it compulsory for all ingermane mutants to behave safely and sensibly at all times and to get treatment for their ingermanity at the earliest possible . . .'

Aristotle stopped.

Nobody was listening.

The king had just swept into the banquet hall, followed by several thousand advisers and consultants. The scientists and royal attendants and chefs were all bowing and curtseying and dribbling out little strands of snot as a sign of respect. The senior adviser was whispering to the king.

Oh dear, thought Aristotle.

He didn't like the way the king was looking at him.

The king held up his arms. All of them. The other germs in the room must never have seen all his arms up before, because they fell silent and gazed at them in shock and awe.

'This,' said the king in a regal voice, 'is a perilous hour for our beloved nostril. The forces of darkness have gathered on our doorstep.'

He pointed at Aristotle with one of his arms.

'Evil germs are among us,' he went on. 'Germs who appear to be the same as us, but who hate freedom, peace and friendship. Germs who, despite what they say, have already attacked us with whipped cream.'

The advisers, consultants, scientists, attendants and chefs all gasped.

Aristotle realised they were all looking at him, and not in a friendly way.

The king lowered his other arms until they were all pointing at Aristotle.

'Evil germs,' said the king, 'who have already sent one of their number to spy on us.'

'No,' said Aristotle, before he could stop himself. 'They didn't. I was banished.'

It was too late. Now he'd have to explain.

'I was sent away,' he said quietly. 'For being silly.'

The other germs all stared at him in shocked silence.

'Tragic,' said the king. 'What sort of germs banish one of their own? Not germs like us. Not germs who respect and care for one another. Not germs who love peace and friendship. One day, sure as snot goes hard, this dark empire next door will attack our freedom, attack our peace, attack our nostril. That is why we must strike first.'

The room erupted into cheers.

Aristotle stared at the king in horror.

'No,' he said. 'We're not like that. We're law abiding, just like you. We've got thousands of laws. Millions.'

But the cheering throng couldn't hear him. They weren't listening. They only had noise molecules for the king, who caused even more frenzied cheering with his next words.

'Let Operation Cold War commence.'

Aristotle felt sick.

He knew what war meant. He'd heard the stories. The recent war between the tummy germs and the bottom germs, for example.

Devastation.

And now, thought Aristotle miserably, this nostril's going to attack our nostril.

Another thought smacked into him like an ice chunk from a human's Slurpee.

Oh no.

Blob.

Aristotle had survived the whipped cream, so chances were Blob had too. But would he survive an all-out attack by war-mad neighbours?

Before Aristotle could answer that awful question, he was grabbed by several palace guards.

As they dragged him away, one desperate thought squeezed through the cakes and cat-hair burgers inside his over-stuffed membrane.

I've got to get to Blob, Aristotle said to himself, and warn him.

12

It was the same nostril Blob had known all his life, and yet as he pushed his way through the crowds of nose germs queueing at army recruitment follicles, it felt different.

With a shiver of excitement, Blob knew why.

He'd never escaped from a military hospital before.

Never bounced on a bed and out the window before. Never parachuted to the ground clinging to a piece of nightie fluff before. Never put on a fake voice and pretended to be a doctor on his way to play golf before.

It felt good.

So good, he thought, I wouldn't mind doing it again.

But he decided not to risk it. Going back into the hospital would increase his chances of being caught by at least twice. So would escaping again. Which would add up to four times the risk. Or was that eight?

Blob stopped in a quiet alleyway between two blood capillaries and slapped himself with several of his arms.

Calm down, he told himself. If you don't calm down you're going to end up one of the three percent of germs who never get anything finished because they keep getting overexcited.

He counted up to ten thousand.

Quickly, but it still helped.

That was better. Now he could focus on his mission. Finding Aristotle and getting him to safety before the other nostril was obliterated by the wind of peace and freedom.

In the other nostril, Aristotle clung to the ceiling of the dungeon with all his arms and legs.

'Come on,' he muttered.

His arms and legs were aching.

He wished the dungeon guard would hurry up and arrive with lunch so he could drop from the ceiling onto the guard, overpower the guard, take the guard's keys, lock the guard in the dungeon, disguise himself in the guard's cap, and find a way back home in time to warn Blob and the others that they were going to be invaded and killed, so they'd better be on their guard.

It's a good plan, thought Aristotle.

He was a little concerned about some parts of it, though.

The overpowering bit, for example.

He'd never actually overpowered anyone before. Not in real life. Specially not a trained dungeon guard.

Then there was the cap. What if it didn't fit? Or it turned out dungeon guards didn't have caps?

But the part of the plan that worried Aristotle most was the lunch part. He'd just spent quite a bit of time in the banquet hall telling everyone how bloated and full up and incapable of eating another thing he was.

Would they be giving him lunch so soon?

Ever?

'Pssst.'

Aristotle almost fell off the ceiling. He looked around to see where the voice was coming from. And when he saw, he almost fell off the ceiling again.

Standing in the gloom at the other end of the dungeon were several big weird-shaped multi-coloured microbes. One of them was square and yellow with blue arms and legs.

Aristotle stared.

'Ralph?' he said in amazement.

'No,' said the big square yellow microbe, looking amazed too. 'Ralph's my brother. He got breathed into the other nostril when I got breathed into this one. You know Ralph?'

Aristotle explained to Ralph's brother how Ralph had taught him everything he knew about telling a chunk of talcum powder from a lump of gnat's dandruff.

'Well you'd better come down here then,' said Ralph's brother. 'If you want to get back to your nostril that is.'

Aristotle slid painfully down the dungeon wall and over to the microbes.

'Here,' said Ralph's brother. 'Try this.'

Aristotle couldn't believe what he was seeing. Ralph's brother was holding open a tissue paper flap revealing a hole in the wall of the dungeon.

'We've been working on this for a while,' he said. 'It's not big enough for us yet, but a little squirt like you should fit through.'

'Thanks,' said Aristotle. 'I don't know what to say.'

'When you see Ralph,' said his brother, 'tell him Lou's on his way.'

'I will,' said Aristotle. 'Thank you so much.'

He was tempted to stay and help Lou and the others make the hole big enough for them too, but then he remembered that if he didn't get home soon and warn Blob and Ralph and the others about the invasion, there wouldn't be any point.

'Thanks,' said Aristotle again and wriggled into the hole.

Blob hadn't been this far up the back of the nostril since he was a little kid on a pimple-counting trip.

He crouched behind a skin blemish and looked around.

All clear.

As he'd hoped, there wasn't a nostril defence

force border guard to be seen. They were all busy at the recruiting stations, signing up millions of new recruits for the invasion of the other nostril.

Blob could see a queue from here. He was tempted to count the recruits. He didn't. Well, only the first six hundred and forty-two.

Then he slapped himself a couple of times and crept fearfully into the dark tunnel at the end of the nostril.

It was at moments like this he most wished he had a parent. A wise loving parent who would hug him and tell him important things he needed to know. Like whether you could get into the other nostril by this back way. And what was the chance, expressed as a percentage, of being attacked by scary monster germs in a dark tunnel like this.

While he crept through the gloom, Blob kept his spirits up by counting every germ he could remember who had ever been to the other nostril by the back way.

His spirits didn't stay up for long.

The total was zero.

But Blob kept going.

I may not have a parent, he thought sadly, but I do have a brother.

Or rather he hoped he still did.

Aristotle stood frozen with fear.

Everything had been going so well.

The tunnel from the dungeon had led into a

dried-out capillary and Aristotle had been making really good time along the inside of the smooth old blood vessel until just now when he'd heard footsteps running after him.

For a moment he'd assumed it was Lou and the others.

Then he'd smelled the awful whiff of half-digested bacon and rotting spinach and that human food that comes in red boxes.

Aristotle knew exactly what the smell meant.

A tummy germ.

Aristotle remembered everything Blob had ever said about tummy germs. How they're bigger than nose germs. How they live much longer. Oh, and the stuff about them being cruel vicious killers. Aristotle trembled, his insides tight with fear.

Then he turned round to face his pursuer.

'G'day,' said the tummy germ. 'Lou asked me to point you in the right direction.'

Aristotle had to admit the tummy germ didn't look like a crazed killer.

Not completely.

OK, it did have a very tough-looking acid-proof outer layer. And it did have the sharpest most vicious-looking claws Aristotle had ever seen. But as it stood there nodding at Aristotle, it was definitely grin-shaped.

'Thanks,' said Aristotle. He pointed along the capillary in the direction he'd been going. 'Isn't this the right direction?'

'Not any more,' said the tummy germ. 'Carry on along there and you'll end up in the sinuses. You want to go this way.'

With a sudden movement that made Aristotle flinch and jump back, the tummy germ slashed a hole in the wall of the capillary with one of its fearsome claws.

Aristotle wondered if he was going to be kidnapped and taken down to the tummy and dissolved in acid. He thought about trotting for it. Then he thought about what would happen to Blob if he didn't get back home soon and warn everyone.

The tummy germ peered out through the jagged hole in the capillary and signalled for Aristotle to do the same.

'See that big tunnel at the back of the nostril,' said the tummy germ. 'That's the way to your nostril.'

Suddenly the tummy germ grabbed Aristotle and pulled him back into the capillary.

Aristotle caught a glimpse of a royal commando platoon marching past.

'Don't want to get picked up by them,' muttered the tummy germ.

'I know,' said Aristotle grimly. 'Thanks.'

He peeked out of the hole again and studied the dark tunnel at the end of the nostril.

'Hope we don't meet any in there,' he said.

'I won't,' said the tummy germ. 'This is as far as I go. You're on your own from here.'

Aristotle looked at the tummy germ.

'You're not going back to the tummy?' he said.

'Nope,' said the tummy germ. 'My place is up here, keeping an eye on these dodgy nose germs. No offence. Lou explained you're different. But you lot have already wiped each other out several times, and we're worried you might get bored with that and start on us.'

Aristotle stared at the tummy germ.

'What do you mean?'

'You nostrils invade each other and wipe each other out on a regular basis,' said the tummy germ. 'It's happened twice already in my lifetime and I'm only two weeks old.'

Aristotle struggled to take this in.

'Of course,' continued the tummy germ, 'you don't wipe each other out completely. There's always a few survivors in each nostril to start a new population. But the poor buggers are in such shock, they never remember what's happened. And so the whole thing starts all over again. Which is why my job is to lie low here and warn the folks at home if I see an invasion brewing. I wish your silly leaders could grasp just how predictable you lot are. Present company excepted.'

Aristotle knew the first thing he'd be doing once he found his way back home.

'Don't worry,' he said. 'I'm going back to tell them now.'

'Good luck, mate,' said the tummy germ.

'Thanks,' said Aristotle. 'Thanks for everything.'

With a cheery wave, the tummy germ set off back along the capillary. And reappeared a moment later.

'One thing I forgot to tell you,' it said. 'When you get to the other end of that tunnel, there's a big open paddock. The tunnel to your nostril leads off it. But there's something else in the paddock you have to watch out for. Millions and millions of sneeze cells. Do you know what sneeze craters look like?'

'No,' said Aristotle.

'Well, be careful,' said the tummy germ. 'If you irritate them, the human will sneeze and we'll all be blasted out of the nose to certain death. See ya.'

The tummy germ headed off again.

Sneeze cells, thought Aristotle.

He felt like retreating along the capillary with the tummy germ.

But he didn't. He had a job to do and no time to waste hanging around being scared. If he wanted to feel scared, he'd have to do it on the move.

Aristotle scrambled through the jagged hole onto the nostril floor and peered around.

All clear.

As he'd hoped, the royal commando border guards weren't even at their posts. They were busy at the recruiting stations, signing up millions of new recruits for the invasion of his and Blob's nostril.

Aristotle hurried into the dark tunnel.

While he crept through the gloom, he kept

his spirits up by thinking about all the interesting experiences he'd had lately.

Finding a second nostril.

Meeting a king and Ralph's brother.

Discovering that not all tummy germs are deranged killers.

Learning some very important facts from history.

The only disappointing experience, thought Aristotle, was when the scientists couldn't discover why I'm so different.

He didn't let it get him down. In fact, as he hurried on through the darkness, he made a plan.

Study hard.

Become a doctor.

Find out myself why I'm different.

It felt like a good plan.

But first he had to save Blob and all the others from the coming war.

13

The big open paddock at the end of the tunnel was exactly like the tummy germ had said.

Big.

Open.

Full of sneeze cells.

At first, Aristotle had trouble recognising them.

The paddock was vast, almost as big as the forest territory north of the human's top lip. But there was no pale-coloured skin hair here. Just row after row of fleshy ridges, bare except for millions of little craters.

The craters looked empty.

Aristotle had started tiptoeing between them when he felt the wind change direction. It was blowing in through the nostril now.

Or rather, thought Aristotle grimly, nostrils.

Floating on the wind was a big fluff ball. It wasn't big enough to be nightie fluff. Aristotle peered at it as it tumbled past.

Cotton bud fluff?

Dandelion fluff?

No, he decided when he'd had a good squiz at it. Butterfly fluff. It built up in their bellybuttons, and when they did a heavy landing on a flower or something, it popped out and became airborne.

Aristotle watched as the butterfly bellybutton fluff tumbled into one of the craters.

He saw that the crater wasn't empty after all. A quivering skin cell rose up inside it to meet the fluff. And immediately the whole world started to tremble.

The wind got stronger. The fleshy ridges shook with terrible spasms. Aristotle was thrown to the ground. He lay there, arms and legs wrapped protectively over himself. He was trembling too. Waiting for the sneeze that would hurl him and all the other nose germs into oblivion and wipe out another generation.

But there was no sneeze.

The trembling spasms slowly subsided.

The wind dropped.

The fluff ball, soggy now with mucus, lay harmlessly on the edge of the crater.

Phew, thought Aristotle. That was close.

He picked himself up and tiptoed carefully back to the edge of the paddock, careful not to slip on any of the ridges and fall into any of the craters. He knew that if butterfly bellybutton fluff could almost cause a sneeze, then a germ, even a small one like him, would certainly do it.

When he got to the edge of the paddock and didn't have to watch where he was treading any more, he looked up. And saw, in the distance, at the other end of the paddock, another tunnel.

The back entrance to another nostril.

My nostril, thought Aristotle.

He went sad and happy shaped at the same time which hurt. Then he saw something that made him forget the pain.

A tiny figure, standing at the other end of the paddock, waving to him and shouting something.

'Blob,' yelled Aristotle, jumping into the air and waving back with delight.

He stopped almost immediately.

Germs who jumped and waved, specially excited ones, could easily fall into sneeze craters.

'Be careful,' he yelled to Blob. 'There are sneeze cells everywhere.'

Blob was still shouting something, but the breeze was carrying his words away and Aristotle didn't have a clue what he was saying.

Aristotle looked around for a safe way to get to Blob.

He saw that on each side of the paddock was a high cliff. On the cliffs were narrow ledges that didn't seem to have sneeze craters on them.

'Hang on,' Aristotle yelled to Blob. 'I'll come to you.'

He clambered up onto the highest ledge he could

see, the one that was the safest distance from the sneeze cells, and started making his way carefully along the cliff towards Blob.

It was going to take a while, but Aristotle knew Blob would have plenty to keep himself occupied. Counting the sneeze craters, for a start.

The ledge was very narrow. Aristotle had to keep all his attention on where he was walking. If he slipped and rolled down into a sneeze crater . . .

He stopped for a rest and peered ahead towards Blob.

Who wasn't there.

Aristotle went panic-shaped.

Had Blob slipped and rolled down?

Phew. No, he hadn't. There he was, on a lower ledge, making his way along the cliff towards Aristotle.

I wish you'd stay put, thought Aristotle, going anxious-shaped. With your hopeless balance, there's at least a ten to ninety percent chance you'll fall off.

He pushed the thought away and tried to replace it with a less anxious one.

We're heading towards each other.

Soon we'll be together again.

'Blob,' yelled Aristotle, waving. 'Be careful. Don't try and go too fast.'

Blob yelled and waved back.

Aristotle still couldn't hear what he was saying. He seemed to be pointing towards the tunnel that Aristotle had recently come out of. And he was trotting along the narrow ledge much too quickly.

'Slow down,' yelled Aristotle. 'Stop and count to a million.'

Blob was gesticulating even more wildly now, using all his arms and even a couple of his legs as he trotted.

Aristotle glanced back over his shoulder at the tunnel Blob was getting so excited about. And instantly saw why.

Speeding out of the tunnel was a platoon of royal commandos. They started to jump up onto Aristotle's ledge.

'Down here stupid commandos,' yelled Blob. 'I'll pulverise you all.'

The commandos dropped down onto the lower ledge and headed straight for Blob.

'Go back,' Aristotle yelled frantically to Blob. 'Head for our nostril.'

But Blob didn't go back. He trotted at full speed, Aristotle saw with horror, straight at the advancing commandos.

As he got closer, Aristotle could finally hear what he was saying.

'Look out,' Blob was yelling. 'They're coming from both directions.'

That's when Aristotle noticed the other troops, a platoon of government soldiers, coming out of the tunnel he was heading towards.

Aristotle knew he should be relieved. These troops were from his nostril. They were on his side. They could rescue Blob. But there was something about the way they were rushing towards him instead of Blob that made Aristotle feel sick and anxious.

Blob crashed into the royal commandos, flailing at them with all his arms and legs, trying to fight them.

He was, Aristotle saw, losing badly.

The commandos were picking him up and carrying him off.

Aristotle, yelling, frantic, tried to climb down to help him, but the ledge was too high.

I don't understand, thought Aristotle numbly as he dangled off the ledge. Blob must have known he couldn't defeat a whole platoon of commandos. He must have done the maths.

'Why didn't you let them take me?' Aristotle yelled at Blob. 'I'm the one they're after.'

The commandos were just about to carry Blob into their tunnel, but Blob managed to twist around and yell a few words.

Aristotle could barely make out what he was saying.

It sounded a bit like, 'Because you're my brother.'

Then the government troops grabbed Aristotle and started dragging him towards the tunnel he'd been heading for all along, except now Aristotle wasn't pleased to be going there at all.

14

The prime minister gave a big sigh.

Aristotle could see he wasn't happy. His big think molecules were moving in a very depressed and miserable sort of way.

In fact, Aristotle was noticing that none of the germs at home seemed very happy.

One clue was the way the troops were throwing him carelessly onto the floor in the government meeting room. Another was the way they were leaving him there tied up with very strong rope, the sort made from cockroach eyelashes. Then there was the fact that not one of the government ministers was offering to untie him.

Aristotle hoped everyone would be much more positive and energetic once he'd mentioned Blob.

'They've got him,' said Aristotle desperately. 'Blob. We must rescue him.'

'I'm sorry,' said the prime minister quietly, 'but

we have more important things to worry about.'

'Please,' said Aristotle. 'He's my brother.'

The minister for defence glared grimly down at Aristotle.

'Our battle plan,' he said. 'Operation Nosewipe. What do those heathens next door know about it?'

Aristotle decided to tell them everything he knew. And then perhaps they'd rescue Blob.

'It's all happened before,' said Aristotle. 'All this. At least twice in the last two weeks. Before any of us were born.'

Aristotle could see that the minister for defence wasn't listening.

'Do they know our attack route?' demanded the minister.

Aristotle sighed.

'Please, listen to me,' he said. 'We're repeating history. And it always ends in disaster.'

All the government ministers and military officers in the room frowned and threw each other puzzled glances.

'He's in shock,' said the minister for defence.

'He's even sillier than usual,' said the prime minister.

'No, I'm not, honest,' said Aristotle.

The minister for defence leaned even closer.

'You're in very big trouble, young germ,' he said. 'So if you want to save the nostril of your birth you'd better tell us now the exact numbers of the enemy armed forces. That's the exact number of military, the exact number of support units and the exact number, in total, of germs bearing arms.'

Aristotle looked helplessly up at the ministers.

'Um . . .' he said. 'Lots?'

The prime minister stepped forward again.

'Listen carefully, you silly germ,' he said. 'Our survival depends on this, including yours. Is there anything at all you can tell us that will help us in our strike against the enemy?'

Aristotle thought desperately for something he could tell them, something that would help Blob. They wouldn't listen to the truth about their history, so it had to be something else.

Of course.

Why hadn't he thought of it before?

'I know one thing,' he said. 'You mustn't attack them the back way.'

'Sneeze cells?' said the king, looking puzzled.

Blob nodded.

He was so awed, he was finding it a bit hard to speak. He'd never been in the presence of a king before, not even a puzzled one. And this palace was incredible. He couldn't begin to count how many bits of how many tissues had been used to build the ornate walls and ceilings.

'We know nothing about any sneeze cells,' said an important-looking adviser to the king.

'There are millions of them,' said Blob. 'That's why you mustn't attack by the back way.'

He squinted pleadingly up at the adviser, who was the strangest-shaped germ he'd ever seen.

Maybe it's just my squiz molecules playing up, thought Blob. Probably be a sixty percent chance of that when you're lying on the floor like this tied up very tightly with very strong rope made from dust-mite armpit hair.

'This is just great,' the king was saying bitterly. 'First everyone forgets my birthday, now there are millions of sneeze cells covering our attack route.'

Blob watched as the royal adviser's strange-shaped bulges twitched long-sufferingly.

'May I remind you, your majesty,' he said, 'that this young germ is a replacement enemy spy for the one that escaped. His job is to try and delay us in our quest for peace and freedom. The chances of him telling the truth are about one nothingth of nought percent.'

'Actually,' said Blob, 'it's better to express that either as a fraction or as a percentage.'

The strange-shaped royal adviser went an even stranger shape and gave Blob an angry glare. Then he turned to a large aroma worker who was standing very close to Blob.

'This is your last chance to save your career, Leonard,' said the strange-shaped royal adviser. 'Tell his majesty I'm right.'

The large aroma worker bent down very close to Blob. His expression, Blob saw, rapidly became very pained.

Maybe he's got a bad back, thought Blob.

'Um . . .' said Len. 'The young germ's telling the truth.'

The strange-shaped royal adviser looked as though he was going to explode and splatter them all with his insides. Which Blob didn't think would be a very good thing to do to a king.

'You're fired,' the royal adviser yelled at the aroma worker. Then he turned to the king. 'If we wait, your majesty, we run the risk of them attacking us first.'

'You're right,' said the king. 'I'm ordering the attack now.'

Everyone in the room started scurrying around. Everyone except Blob and the large aroma worker.

Blob couldn't scurry because he was still tied up. He struggled against the ropes but it was no good. Then he noticed how upset the large aroma worker was looking.

So upset that Blob started to think he must have a brother about to be killed in the attack too.

'Sneeze cells?' said the prime minister, looking suspicious.

Aristotle nodded.

'We've never heard anything about any sneeze cells,' said the minister for defence.

'I think I might have once,' said the minister for the environment.

'I've actually seen them,' said Aristotle. 'Butterfly bellybutton fluff sets them off.'

The prime minister and all the other ministers looked at Aristotle and at the minister for the environment.

'So here's our choice,' said the prime minister gravely. 'With a hostile enemy possibly about to attack us at any moment, we can either believe the word of the silliest germ in this nostril . . .'

'And the silliest minister,' said the minister for defence, still glaring at the minister for the environment.

'. . . or,' said the prime minister, 'we can defend ourselves.'

'Defend ourselves,' roared all the other ministers.

'I'm ordering the attack,' said the prime minister.

Everyone in the room started scurrying around.

Everyone except Aristotle and the minister for the environment.

Aristotle couldn't scurry because he was still tied up. He struggled against the ropes but it was no good. Then he noticed how upset the minister for the environment was looking.

So upset that Aristotle started to think he must have a brother about to be killed in the attack too.

15

Aristotle couldn't believe it.

Banished again.

He stood, disbelief-shaped, where the defence force border guards had left him, outside the front entrance to the nostril. He was dimly aware he'd been standing there for ages. Nearly a minute probably.

Thoughts churning.

Insides churning too.

In front of him the whipped-cream covered forest was slowly thawing. Aristotle could see that most of the cream had been licked away, probably by the human or one of its pets. But great globs of it were still dripping from the face hairs, and huge drifts were still glistening in the larger skin cracks.

A germ could get through, thought Aristotle as he peered at the forest.

If he was careful.

And determined.

And then, if he was even more determined,

he could enrol in university and study hard and become a doctor and do research and discover why he was different.

Aristotle knew it wouldn't be easy.

Human universities probably didn't feel so good about germs enrolling. Not in medicine. And the study would be very hard. The medical text books would be very difficult to get through, particularly for a germ who'd keep getting lost in the middle of full stops and would probably keep falling into the cracks where the corners of pages had been folded over.

Still, thought Aristotle, I'd give it a go if I could.

But he knew he couldn't.

Not with history about to repeat itself. Not with a huge battle about to take place at the back of the nostrils. Not with two vast armies about to trample on the sneeze cells. Not with every nose germ in the human about to be blasted out of the nose to oblivion and probable death.

Including Blob.

Aristotle went determined-shaped.

Luckily he had another plan.

It's not going to be easy to pull off, he thought grimly, and some would probably say it's very silly, but that's not going to stop me trying.

The more Blob saw of the vast royal army as it marched towards the back of the nostril, the more sick and anxious he felt.

He knew he couldn't see all of it, which made him feel even worse.

It wasn't easy for a germ to see a whole army when it was that vast. And when he was tied up and being carried over the shoulder of a commando.

'One million two hundred and eight thousand,' Blob murmured to himself, 'six hundred and fifty-three . . . six hundred and fifty-four . . . six hundred and fifty-five . . .'

He stopped counting.

This was pointless.

The army was vast and it was heading for the tunnel at the end of the nostril. Once it was through the tunnel it would be all over the sneeze cell paddock and then everything would be all over.

Unless, thought Blob desperately, I can stop this war.

'Excuse me,' he yelled. 'Your majesty.'

The king, who was being carried nearby on the backs of several royal attendants, glared down at Blob.

'What?' he said tersely.

Blob could see that the king was stressed. War probably did that to a monarch. And there was a ninety-nine point nine percent chance his majesty was still upset that his birthday had been forgotten. He'd been muttering about it the whole march.

Blob pressed on anyway.

'Your majesty,' he said. 'Do you have a Litter Prohibition Act in this nostril?'

'Of course we do,' said the king.

'And a Tidy Nostril Enforcement Bill,' added the senior royal adviser, who was being carried alongside the king.

'I thought so,' said Blob. 'This being such a tidy and law-abiding nostril.'

'Thank you,' said the king.

'You do realise,' said Blob, 'that this war is going to break both those laws. It's going to create a huge amount of litter. You know, food wrappers, drink containers, body parts.'

The king and the senior adviser didn't reply.

It's working, thought Blob.

The senior adviser gave a very big sigh.

Perhaps not, thought Blob

'For us,' said the senior adviser, 'this war is a major clean up. Those germs in the other nostril who hate peace and freedom, we're cleaning them out.'

'Well put,' said the king.

Blob flopped back on the commando's shoulder, defeated.

All he could hope now was that Aristotle had managed to get very far away from the awfulness that was about to happen.

Aristotle was almost ready to go back into the nostril.

Getting everything together hadn't been easy.

The hardest was finding the talcum powder

and playground dust for the cake. He'd searched everywhere around the nostril entrance and had almost given up, but then he'd found some lodged in a crevice in the nostril wall near the abandoned defence force border security post.

Making the cake was hard too.

The kitchen facilities at the border security post were pathetic. The guards were all on their way to the battle, so Aristotle couldn't even ask them if they had a cake whisk.

But now it was done.

Fluffy skin-flake icing.

Carbon molecule candles.

Time to go.

Aristotle turned to face the cool breeze blowing into the nostril. He looked up. And saw exactly what he hoped he'd see.

Butterfly bellybutton fluff, floating into the nostril on the wind.

He reached up and grabbed onto it.

All he could hope now was that he wasn't too late.

16

Blob couldn't bear to look.

The two huge armies were assembling. Each was at its own end of the vast paddock. Each was well away from the sneeze craters.

For now.

OK, he was looking.

He couldn't bear not to.

Because any moment, Blob knew, the king was going to give the order to attack, and millions of germs were going to charge, and then shortly after that they'd start falling into the sneeze craters, and then it would all be over.

For ever.

OK, there was another possibility. That the prime minister would give the order to attack from the other end first.

Probably a fifty percent chance of that, thought Blob grimly. But still with a hundred percent certainty of us all being sneezed to death.

The one good thing was that he couldn't see any sign of Aristotle up the other end.

What a relief.

Aristotle must have got away.

Blob wondered if he should say something to the commando carrying him. It might be the last nice thing he ever had a chance to say to anyone.

He tapped the commando on the shoulder.

'Thanks for the lift,' he said. 'I appreciate it.'

The commando grunted.

Oh well, thought Blob, a grunt's better than nothing.

He wished he could hear Aristotle's voice one more time. Aristotle wouldn't sign off with a grunt. A joke, more like. Or a song. Or a silly idea for making someone happy.

Suddenly Blob found himself wishing that his life had been different. That he'd been more like Aristotle. That he hadn't spent quite so much time counting things and being neat and tidy and worrying about rules and regulations and whether his legs were all the same length.

I wish I'd been a bit more relaxed and easy-going, he thought sadly as he gazed upwards past the commando's top bits. Like that butterfly bellybutton fluff up there.

Blob gazed up at the wisp of fluff blowing on the breeze high above.

That fluff, he thought, doesn't care how many troops there are down here. Six million four hundred thousand two hundred and eleven. Six million four hundred thousand two hundred and twelve.

It couldn't give a fluff.

It's just content to float and be happy.

Then Blob saw that even butterfly bellybutton fluff can have things weighing it down sometimes.

Responsibilities.

Other things.

Blob stared.

Was that a germ hanging off that fluff? Clinging onto it desperately? Carrying a cake?

It was.

And not, Blob saw as he went stunned-shaped, just any germ.

Aristotle was having trouble steering the fluff.

He'd worked out how to turn right and left by leaning all his body weight one way or the other. That was going well as long as he didn't lean too far and drop the cake.

The problem was going to be steering the fluff downwards.

Now that Aristotle had emerged from the wind tunnel at the end of the nostril, he could see the armies massed below at either end of the sneeze-cell paddock.

He could see the prime minister at one end.

He could see the king at the other end.

He knew exactly where he needed to go.

Down.

But how?

Suddenly Aristotle had an idea. He knew if Blob was up here with him, Blob could tell him how many fluff strands were keeping him up. Several million, probably, each with air molecules floating around it.

Blob would also tell him something else.

Ninety percent less strands, ninety percent less up.

Thanks Blob, thought Aristotle.

He kept gripping the cake with a couple of arms and kept hanging on to the fluff with a couple more. With the rest of his arms and all of his legs he wrapped himself around the fluff strands and squeezed tight.

The fluff strands bunched and lost some of their floatiness.

Aristotle waited until he was directly above the king, then squeezed even harder.

The fluff started to descend.

Yes, thought Aristotle.

The fluff started to plummet.

Oh no, thought Aristotle.

It wasn't so bad. Aristotle hit the ground hard, but the two other things he'd been hoping for were fine. He hit the ground directly in front of the king, and he didn't smash the cake.

Aristotle stood up and faced the king. He knew he had to be quick. The king's troops were moving towards him. They were assuming it was an aerial attack.

Which in a way, thought Aristotle, it is.

'Happy birthday, your majesty,' he said in the loudest voice he could. 'I bring you this birthday cake from our nostril, with our best wishes for many happy returns, and our apologies for the misunderstanding that has brought us all here.'

The king was staring at Aristotle, dumbfounded.

Then he went grin-shaped.

'At last,' said the king. 'Someone has not only remembered my birthday, they've done it seven minutes early.'

He gave a meaningful stare at his advisers and consultants and attendants, who all looked ill and like they wished they weren't there.

Aristotle glanced anxiously at the king's troops. And was relieved to see the king signalling to them to hold back.

'Sorry we missed your last birthday,' said Aristotle. 'Fifty-three minutes ago our nostril didn't know your nostril existed, so we couldn't give anything to you then.'

Aristotle held the cake out to the king.

The king beamed at it.

Aristotle started singing as loudly as he could.

'Happy birthday to you . . .'

For a while he was singing on his own. Then another voice joined in. A voice that Aristotle recognised.

Blob.

He looked around and saw his brother, tied up

and flopped over the shoulder of a commando, singing fit to bust.

Blob saw him and they both went grin-shaped.

Then the whole world started to tremble.

The wind got stronger. The fleshy ridges across the paddock shook with terrible spasms. Troops were being thrown to the ground. Millions of voices started screaming. Millions of arms and legs were wrapped protectively over millions of trembling outer membranes.

Aristotle looked around in panic.

And saw that the butterfly bellybutton fluff had tumbled into one of the sneeze craters.

Aristotle stuffed the cake into the king's hands.

He danced and skipped desperately between the craters until he got to the one with the fluff ball in it. He grabbed the fluff ball and dragged it off the quivering skin membrane. He smothered the fluff ball with his body and waited, trembling, for the sneeze that would fling him and all the other nose germs into oblivion and make history repeat itself.

But there was no sneeze.

The trembling spasms slowly subsided.

The wind dropped.

And from over near the king, Aristotle heard a single voice still singing.

'Happy birthday to you . . .'

Good on you, Blob, thought Aristotle as he went carefully to the edge of the paddock.

He joined in, but this time he and Blob weren't

singing alone for long. The king's advisers and consultants and attendants joined in, then the king's troops, and then, down the other end, the prime minister's troops.

The great open paddock, the meeting place of the two nostrils, rang with millions of trembling grateful voices.

And, as Aristotle looked around and saw that every germ in the place was relief-shaped, he had the strangest but most wonderful feeling.

The germs weren't just singing in praise of the king's birthday, they were also singing in gratitude to Aristotle and Blob.

17

Blob's whole body went grin-shaped as he thought about the very good thing he was about to do.

He peered around the crowded nostril.

The other germs were all busy. Some were giving each other piggybacks. Others were sliding down nose-hair highways. Or bouncing on mucus trampolines. Or welcoming tourists and exchange students from the other nostril.

There was Aristotle's friend the tummy germ, giving the government ministers a history lesson.

This was the perfect moment.

Blob grabbed his brother and dragged him behind a chunk of broken-off nose hair.

'Hey,' complained Aristotle. 'Don't. I'm trying to teach the king how to play table tennis. I think he's wishing he hadn't asked for a table-tennis table for his birthday. The prime minister's beating him eight hundred and forty-seven to nil.'

Blob knew it probably wasn't as many as that,

but he didn't care. He could see that the senior royal adviser had taken over the lesson and was showing the king how to do backhand. Which wasn't bad considering the adviser had several little kids clambering over his bulges.

'Surprise,' said Blob happily.

He pointed to the birthday cake sitting on a pimple.

Aristotle stopped struggling and went grin-shaped. He looked at the cake, at the candles, at the very neat icing, and then at his brother.

'We're twelve,' said Blob.

'Thank you,' said Aristotle. 'Happy birthday.'

They gave each other a long hug.

Then Aristotle looked around his nostril. At the defence force troops playing soccer against the royal commandos. At Ralph and Lou and the other visiting microbes showing kids how to juggle chunks of gnat dandruff. At Len, sniffing the chief judge and not being arrested. At Blob cutting the birthday cake and not even counting the candles.

The nostril, he saw, was full of happy germs.

Millions of them.

Suddenly Aristotle didn't feel so different after all.

EXTRA TIME

A young Aussie soccer genius and his
10-year-old manager take on the world.
And win. For a time.

TOO SMALL TO FAIL

What do you do when your mum, your dad
and sixteen camels are in trouble – and
only you can save them? The sometimes sad
but mostly funny story of a boy, a girl,
a dog and four trillion dollars.

GRACE

In the beginning there was me and
Mum and Dad and the twins. And talk about
happy families, we were bountiful. But it
came to pass that I started doing sins. And lo,
that's when all our problems began.

LOYAL CREATURES

They were loyal creatures, the men and horses
of the Australian Light Horse, but war doesn't
always pay heed to loyalty. This is the powerful
story of a 16-year-old volunteer and his horse
in World War One and the journey towards
his own kind of bravery.

ONCE

Once I escaped from an orphanage to
find Mum and Dad. Once I saved a girl called
Zelda from a burning house. Once I made a Nazi
with a toothache laugh. My name is Felix.
This is my story.

THEN

I had a plan for me and Zelda. Pretend
to be someone else. Find new parents. Be safe
forever. Then the Nazis came.

AFTER

After the Nazis took my parents I was scared.
After they killed my best friend I was angry.
After they ruined my thirteenth birthday I was
determined. To get to the forest. To join
forces with Gabriek and Yuli. To be a family.
To defeat the Nazis after all.

SOON

I hoped the Nazis would be defeated. And
they were. I hoped the war would be over.
And it was. I hoped we would be safe.
But we aren't.

NOW

Once I didn't know about my grandfather
Felix's scary childhood. Then I found out
what the Nazis did to his best friend Zelda.
Now I understand why Felix does the things
he does. At least he's got me. My name is
Zelda too. This is our story.

BOY OVERBOARD

Jamal and Bibi have a dream. To lead Australia
to soccer glory in the next World Cup. But first
they must face landmines, pirates, storms and
assassins. Can Jamal and his family survive their
incredible journey and get to Australia?

GIRL UNDERGROUND

Bridget wants a quiet life. Including, if possible,
keeping her parents out of prison. Then a boy
called Menzies makes her an offer she can't
refuse and they set off on a job of their own.
It's a desperate, daring plan – to rescue two kids,
Jamal and Bibi, from a desert detention centre.
Can Bridget and Menzies pull off their very
first jail break, or will they end up
behind bars too?

TOAD RAGE

The epic and very funny story of one
slightly squashed cane toad's quest for the truth.

TOAD HEAVEN

The stirring saga of one slightly squashed
cane toad's dreams of a safe place and what
happens when he wakes up.

TOAD AWAY

The heroic tale of one slightly squashed
cane toad's travels across oceans, continents
and some really busy roads.

TOAD SURPRISE

The wart-tingling escapade of one slightly
squashed cane toad's hunt for friendship and
the surprising place he finds it.

GIFT OF THE GAB

It's a normal week for Rowena Batts.
A car full of stewed apples. A police cell.
A struggle to keep Dad off national TV.
Then her world turns upside down.

TEACHER'S PET

Ginger is allergic to cats.
And possibly to her family as well.
She's also not keen on the cat food in her breakfast
bowl or the school principal trying to kill her
best friend. The question on everyone's
lips is – will Ginger snap?

THE OTHER FACTS OF LIFE

Ben stared at the TV. He'd never seen anything like
it. Fascinating. Incredible. Awful. He had to do
something.

WATER WINGS

Pearl needs a gran and she needs one now.
Luckily she's got Winston to help her.
You can do anything when your best friend
is the world's brainiest guinea pig.
Well, almost anything.

ADULTS ONLY

Jake is an only kid. He's the only kid in his family.
He's the only kid on his island.
Or that's what he thinks.

BUMFACE

His mum calls him Mr Dependable,
but Angus can barely cope. Another baby
would be a disaster. So Angus comes up with
a bold and brave plan to stop her getting
pregnant. That's when he meets Rindi.
And Angus thought *he* had problems . . .

WORM STORY

Wilton has a bad feeling in his tummy.
The one he lives in. Can one worm discover new
worlds and save his friends from destruction?
Wilton is about to find out.

SECOND CHILDHOOD

Mark and his friends discover they've lived before.
Not only that – they were Famous and Important
People! Which is lots of fun. At first.

ABOUT THE AUTHOR

Morris Gleitzman grew up in England and came to Australia when he was sixteen. After university he worked for ten years as a screenwriter. Then he had a wonderful experience. He wrote a novel for young people. Now, after 36 books, he's one of Australia's most popular children's authors.

VISIT MORRIS AT HIS WEBSITE:
www.morrisgleitzman.com